BEYOND BEAUTY

BEYOND BEAUTY

by

Vernon Nelson

BEYOND BEAUTY

BEYOND BEAUTY

by

Vernon Nelson

Table of Contents

CHAPTER 1 - Discovery

It was a freezing winter morning deep in the middle of nowhere; the nowhere of the Texas woods that is. The wind chill was relentless at this time of year - so relentless you could still feel it biting you to the core no matter how warmly you dressed. The spacious forest was almost entirely covered with snow and the subtle hints of greenery were barely visible.

Snowflakes were falling icily from the sky, vanishing instantly with each impact against the ground. Behind the screen of free-falling snow, roughly a half-mile ahead, something became more noticeable; a luxurious cabin-styled lake house. So mysterious and elegant it looked as the breeze blew fiercely over the top of it. The sound of the violent wind swooshing against it proved enough to send shivers along the spines of the strongest of men.

The entire scene looked like something out of a horror movie. Nearly too perfect; it made you wonder if the lake house was even real or if you were on the location of an extravagant film-shoot. Still, no amount of rationalization could reduce the air of mystery it radiated.

A stray leaf, buried halfway beneath the snow, began to emerge more clearly as small speckles of the ice melted away. It ascended and then hovered leisurely in mid-air. The wind held it there for a moment before it began drifting. It drifted for a while, changing its direction several times, before finally resting gently against a glass window of the lake house.

Inside sat a woman with long dark hair playing the piano; completely lost in her music. You could tell how passionate she was about playing by the way her fingers glided over, and eloquently pressed into, the keys. She was wearing a sheer veil similar to the hijab that Middle Eastern women wore but this one was different. Beneath this one you were still able to capture a glimpse of how attractive she was. Her dark, almond-shaped eyes and long lashes brought attention to how unique and exotic her features were. Her lean curvaceous frame sat perfectly postured as her hands maneuvered gently along the piano's keyboard; it was one of the things that made her feel beautiful. After all that was her name; Beauty...

Beauty had been living in the deep, quiet woods at the lake house since she was 25 years old; that was when her husband Robert tragically lost his struggle with cancer at the young age of only 35 years.

Robert had built this place for Beauty with his bare hands. It was her dream home and she couldn't bring herself to ever leave it. But ten years had passed now and, at thirty five, she was still alone.

She did have Buddy - a pit bull and tiger mix that Robert had bred secretly before he died. Buddy was four and a half feet tall with all four feet on the ground. He was white with black stripes and a strong muscular body. He looked as though a pit bulls' head had been sculpted smoothly onto a tiger's body. He was mean, beautiful, unforgiving to local wildlife, and especially protective of Beauty.

Playing the piano was therapeutic for Beauty; it was her way of escaping thoughts of how lonely and bitter she'd become; though sometimes it did the opposite.

So on occasion she'd find herself so lost in playing that she'd find herself reliving that painful day when Robert died. He'd died in her arms as they sat silently on the honey-colored wooden floor of the lake house.

She often blamed herself; regretting that she had not called a medic that day. Though part of her knew the disease had ran its course and it was just his time to go. Still, she couldn't help wondering – if she *had* made that call, would things be different now?

Every few seconds she'd study her bronze complexion in the mirror wondering if she was still as beautiful as Robert had made her feel.

Beauty was bi-racial. She came from a good family in Egypt. Her mother was Egyptian; her father an African-American from California. Her parents had met at the American university in Cairo. She remembered hearing them say that it was "love at first sight". They had been married twenty years when her father brought them to the United States and it was nothing short of a culture shock when they realized the freedoms to be had in America.

Beauty had attained her nursing degree in New York, moved around a little, and finally settled in the piney woods of East Texas with Robert where he built their home.

Robert found both fame and fortune as a successful author but his past was not without question. He had spent 12 years in prison for two robberies committed in his youth. That's where they'd met - in prison.

After Beauty graduated from nursing school she decided to take some time off and her quest for relaxation and change brought her to the bright city lights of Las Vegas.

She remembered, as if it were yesterday, the night she met Marissa, one of the nurses who worked at the nearby prison. They were having drinks at the Venetian when Marissa told her about an opening at the prison and how she could get her the job. Marissa was half Egyptian and half black, the same as Beauty, so their chance meeting soon begat a sisterhood between them.

It wasn't long before Beauty found her way to the prison. There was an hour-long orientation, mostly concerning security measures. Her presence at the prison put everyone on edge because she looked as though she belonged on someone's runway or in a beauty pageant somewhere with her long legs and perfectly round bottom, not working at a prison. She was absolutely breathtaking. She looked like an Egyptian goddess with her dark hair, dark eyes, and exotic features, not to mention her uniquely complexioned brown skin.

It was no surprise that the women hated her, or that every male guard wanted to be the first to have a shot at this gorgeous exotic import.

Then there were the inmates. Every time she made her rounds to pass out meds, they could be seen standing at attention in their cell-windows, looking, wondering even; who was this stunningly beautiful woman and why was she working here?

Perhaps Beauty even wondered that herself. After all, her family had money. Her father grossed three million dollars a year from real-estate and she was daddy's little girl.

But Beauty was a vibrant, thirty-five year old. She was an adventurous girl and a bit of a humanitarian at heart, so a job like this suited her. It gave her a sense of usefulness and made her feel important; all while finding her own way at the same time.

All men in prison weren't bad. She remembered her uncle Saayid who'd served 10 years in an Egyptian prison for killing a man who'd broken into his house. He was the same uncle who treated her like a princess when she was a little girl; the same uncle prosecutors tried to make spend the rest of his life behind bars.

After a few moments of playing her piano, her mind flickered to the first time she encountered Robert. It was a sunny, summer morning at the prison when she received a call to respond to a location where one of the inmates had been injured. She and Marissa hopped on the medical golf cart and traveled to the unit where the incident had taken place. When they arrived, it was to a sight that made her heart beat faster with apprehension. There were about thirty or so inmates lying face down on the ground, scattered around the prison yard. Most of them were handcuffed with their hands behind their backs. Marissa ordered her to go and help a man lying alone off in the distance.

When she got to him, he was lying on his side turning back and forth. She could hear him moaning and grunting faintly as he tried to control his breathing. His T-shirt was soaked in blood and it was then she realized that he had been shot. She knelt in front of him, looking more carefully. In his eyes she saw the pain that ached in his heart. In his long lashes there were tears that he blinked back; trying to hold them in. But the burning pain was too intense.

His breathing grew fainter and his eyes were dimming. Beauty gazed at his handsome young face trying to think of what to do next. Her eyes wandered up to the cat-walk style gun-rail where there was an officer with a shotgun staring down at the inmate, who was now lying motionless.

"Boo-hoo already, lady; let him go," he said. "The world's a better place without him anyway; we'll save the taxpayers a lot of money."

I'm surrounded by morons and bores, she thought to herself. She quickly turned her head in disgust, and set about trying to revive him. She performed CPR on him for three minutes with no response. Her final, desperate, act was the soft kiss she planted gently to his full lips after she blew the last bit of air into his mouth.

A few long, agonizing moments went by before his eyes blinked open. When their eyes met it was the first time she realized how handsome he was; *perhaps too good-looking,* she thought as she stared at him.

"Do you always look this beautiful at eight something in the morning?" he murmured and then began coughing.

She sighed in relief and giggled with giddiness in her voice. It was almost as if they were in a conspiratorial whisper. Before she knew it, she found herself sitting down with her hand intimately resting on his chest. If you didn't know better you would've thought they were on a picnic somewhere in the middle of a park from the way they stared at each other.

That was the downside Beauty found in playing the piano; replaying these sad images in her mind over and over and remembering how love had eluded her.

It was in the next instant that Buddy stormed in the house making an aggressive growling sound as he paced back and forth and then stopped in front of her, waiting for her attention. When she looked at him, he dropped a man's boot on the floor. She immediately stopped playing - the last note lingered in the air as she held down the key. And then, it went silent; not even Buddy made a sound. Her eyes wandered the room suspiciously as she quietly ushered him off and locked him in her room. She grabbed the shotgun hanging on the wall and tip-toed into the living room; she knew there was an intruder nearby because Buddy never acted that way. She also noticed he didn't have blood around his mouth so whoever it was must have escaped his wrath.

The size 13 boot was indication that it was a large man. She carefully unlocked the door and turned the porch light on while she loaded the rifle; her dark eyes full of revulsion. She put on the sweat-suit hanging on the coat rack and, regaining her position, peeked out the curtain.

She remained silent as she scanned the entryway and there she saw the broad-shouldered, long-haired man dressed in a long sleeved, black turtleneck and dark wrangler jeans. She realized he was missing a boot as he approached slowly on his horse.

He was a well-dressed black man. *What is he doing near the lake house?* She wondered. As soon as he slid off his horse, she closed her eyes and braced herself. The last man that set foot in this house was her husband Robert and there wouldn't be another if she had anything to say or do about it.

She quickly swung open the door as the man began walking towards the house. She aimed the shotgun at the center of his chest. "Don't you take another step," she yelled furiously, adjusting the veil over her face with one hand while holding the rifle steady with the other. Her demeanor was straight forward and warned him to keep his distance. It was as if she were a lioness going against the alpha male.

His body language made it obvious he was uncertain about her. He stopped dead in his tracks with his hands held high in the air; he didn't utter a word or project any fear.

She could see him measuring her with his eyes as if he thought he could take her and that made her nervous. She knew if he charged at her, any error she made might be a fatal one.

"Now, you listen to me real good. I don't know what you're doing here but you've got ten seconds to turn yourself around before I put a load of buckshot in your ass," she blurted.

His facial expression was unreadable but Beauty's dark, fierce eyes burned with anger. It felt like the longest ten seconds of her life.

Within the blink of an eye, he dropped his hands and dove behind her SUV to shield himself.

Beauty's fingertip stalled a moment before she let off four loud consecutive rounds. The sound echoed wickedly through the woods and sent the man's horse stampeding off into the wilderness. And then it went silent; deathly silent.

Her eyes wandered suspiciously for several moments until she finally spotted his feet beneath her SUV. Without warning, four more rounds went flying through the air. But these weren't from Beauty's gun. The mystery man was armed she told herself as she hid behind an old grey statue on the porch. It was then she felt the first true tingle of fear slither down her spine as she pumped out four more rounds.

A few long seconds later, their eyes found each other, meeting through the crevices of what shielded them. Her smoky, dark eyes flared behind the mystery of her veil gazing into his golden-brown eyes.

She could hear Buddy growling and banging furiously against the door and by the sound of it, she knew it wouldn't be long before he came to rescue her.

Their eyes never left each other as they waited to see who would surrender first. Then she saw something. There at the bottom of the SUV, were droplets of his blood seeping into the snow; she had wounded the man. The fear in her eyes momentarily went away as she cautiously walked towards him; the sound of her footsteps crunching in the snow.

There he was lying helpless behind the truck. His eyes were brimming with tears, turning from his side to his back. She could tell his wounds were serious from his quick, short gasps. Her wandering eyes captured his black shirt, soaked in blood.

In the next instant came what sounded like an explosion as Buddy burst through the door and came low-crawling down the porch steps. His beastly growling echoed through the forest as he made his way to the man. Before Beauty knew it, he was standing over the man baring his long fangs.

Death for him was near the man told himself as he clung to the last few breaths he'd take before this hybrid beast sunk its teeth into his neck.

Beauty watched for a few moments. The longer she watched, the more she thought about Robert and the day he lay dying helplessly in that prison yard as life slowly left him.

"Buddy! No!" she yelled loudly. "No," she repeated as he hesitated and backed up a few steps.

It was the first time the man exhaled completely.

Beauty's grip on the long rifle loosened, reluctantly.

"I hoped, perhaps, you would relent a little," he whispered faintly with a hint of a smile.

But Beauty's expression didn't change. She noticed that the man spoke with a British accent; something she hadn't heard in awhile.

"What's your name and what are you doing here?" she asked sharply.

He didn't answer right away.

She could see the waves of faintness coming over him and then briefly subsiding.

"Yes," he uttered panting. "I'll tell you everything - but, I won't live to tell you anything if you don't help me, my lady. Please," he murmured. Desperate, his eyes pleaded for mercy.

When Beauty's eyes roamed across his wounds, she knew he literally had only a few minutes of life left in him. It was the second time in her life she found herself uncertain of what to do next. The first was when Robert died ten years earlier.

How she would ever move on, or recover from that, had become a daily challenge. And now this strange man; closer to death with each moment that passed. Helping him would mean bringing him inside the lake house, something she had promised Robert, as he lay dying in her arms, she would never do.

She debated with herself for several more moments and despite how traitorous she felt, her human heart combined with her natural nurturing desire weakened her; after all, she was a nurse.

The man's eyes began to blur as he watched her walk away and then return moments later. The last thing he saw was her sticking a needle into his arm and then he faded into darkness.

Several hours had gone by before he finally blinked his eyes open slowly adjusting them to the light. The first thing he noticed was the bandage over the right side of his chest and an I.V. in his left arm. Still dazed by the morphine and whatever other drug she had him on, he thought he was in a hospital somewhere; then he saw Beauty leaning against the wall watching him.

Her dark eyes glittered devilishly; eyes so dark that they should've been black. His eyes wandered a little more freely and he spotted the metal bullet sitting on a small silver plate beside the bed; the plate looked like the ones used in a dentist or doctor's office.

"Well," she said sharply as if there was still something unsettling about his mere presence. "What is your name and what are you doing here?"

This time, his words were swift, "Robert; Robert Moses," he said with confidence.

She rolled her eyes in disbelief, clicking her mouth with a blank look on her face. "Now that's got to be the most ridiculous thing I've ever heard."

"Which one - Robert or Moses?" he asked as he shifted and sat upright.

"Moses." she said, tartly, to confuse him. Though in her heart she knew - this was Robert. The only man who's name sent chills up her spine, the only man who made her feel like a silly-giddy girl every time she saw him. Just the thought of his name nearly sent her into the fairytale; the thought of the fairytale-ending she had never received. "And you're doing what here?" she blurted, trying to snap herself out of it.

"Hunting - hunting deer nearby. Unfortunately, it appears I've become the hunted," he said giggling, wincing in pain but with a hint of a smile.

When he said that, her ears focused in on his accent. A black man with a British accent; that's rare, she told herself as a wave of relief came over her.

"Well, hunting stopped two miles back around the spot where you passed the *Do Not Trespass* sign and crossed onto my property." Her comment was more of a question than a statement and Robert picked up on it quickly.

"I am guilty of that, yes - but, I must admit, I am not very much a fan of laws."

The way he said laws with his accent tickled her inside, it was the first time she returned a hint of a smile.

"I do however admire that fine animal you have."

There was a short silence while she watched him in deep thought.

"Truth is I'd followed a deer I'd been stalking onto your property. And just as I was about to take the kill shot, out of nowhere came your loyal servant chasing me up a tree."

And that's how he lost his boot she told herself. "Well Robert," she said in a serious tone as she walked towards him. "I will give you three days to rest and regain your strength - some of it, at least, and then you will be on your way; understood? That means you will leave here and go back to where you came from."

The pain from her words glittered in his eyes. "I'm not here to hurt you lady."

"You will sleep in the guestroom," she interrupted being careful not to give in to his indication for mercy. She had already gone above and beyond what she was comfortable doing. When she started to leave the room, he motioned for her to wait a moment.

She stared at him awkwardly, waiting to hear what he wanted.

"What is your name, might I ask?"

Their eyes met again for a few seconds and this time she wondered if she would tell him the truth; those seconds of wondering were short-lived.

"Beauty," she whispered hesitantly.

A flicker of light shot through his eyes as she turned to the door to leave.

"Beauty," he called out.

She turned around and looked at him as if she already regretted telling him her name. Something told her he'd be taking advantage of calling her that.

"Your name; it suits you," he said.

She nodded halfheartedly and left the room without response.

She was a fighter he thought, "Fire and steel," he whispered before struggling to his feet. He slowly walked down the hallway in the direction she gestured and as he did, his eyes scanned over her beautiful home. From the expensive art hanging on the walls to the luxurious furniture, it was obvious to him that she had created a nice life for herself. That was his last thought before he found himself standing in front of what must be the guestroom. He walked into the darkness, feeling around the wall for the light-switch. But before he could find it, he saw Beauty standing in the doorway holding a lantern that illuminated her face with flickering light.

"Here, take this," she said. "There's no power in this room. I blew the socket out a few months ago and uhh ... well anyway, here." She stated placing the lantern in his hands and leaving the room.

By this time, it was dark outside; that was the first thing he noticed when his eyes drifted out the window. The next thing he noticed was the sound of raindrops resounding against the window as he sat on the bed with his legs stretched out. He wondered how a woman lived alone in such an enormous home. Then, his thoughts went to the lack of electricity in this particular room as he sat in the dim light provided by the lantern.

He was wishing himself far away; so far away that his mind began re-playing the vacation he took to Italy three years before. The late nights he and his friends, Nathan and Tony, spent out on the town chasing women and how easy they had it as men. Oh, how much they loved Americans, he recalled and being part African-American was purely a bonus…

On the dark brick streets of Milan the sound of laughter was nearly drowned out by hip hop and techno music as they exited one club with an entourage of beautiful Italian women and wandered into another. They were quickly escorted upstairs to a V.I.P. room that overlooked a dance floor with five hundred people on it. After a few moments, they settled onto a spacious burgundy, horseshoe-styled couch that accommodated their party of twelve.

There were three guys and nine girls - all brunettes in short, skimpy skirts and cleavage-revealing tops. In front of them was a table holding champagne chilling in a silver ice chest. Nathan and Tony watched and waited to follow Robert's lead – there was no mistake who the alpha ladies' man was - they knew it and so did these women; it was like a silent signal of understanding that seemed to radiate between them.

Robert was plainly 'the man'. He was the most seasoned of the bunch; even though he had the youngest face, he was the oldest of the three men.

Females, young and old, constantly threw themselves at him; they called him beautiful. From his long, lean frame to his perfectly sculpted, sharp-featured face he was the real deal.

And then there were his beautiful eyes, the gold and brown blend that illuminated them from within. His sense of keenness was precise; almost too precise.

Everyone's eyes were on him as he sat back against the burgundy couch.

"Alright, ladies; it's time to smell some sweet, Italian flesh," he said slowly in his accent.

No sooner than he finished speaking, all nine girls stood up and surrounded him; they virtually threw themselves at him. "Me, me," they begged with desperation.

This was the kind of power Robert had over women. This was perhaps the most painful part of the procedure for his friends for they had to watch him hand pick who he wanted first.

"You, darling. Come to me," he said as a flicker of light shot through his eyes.

When she stood in front of him, his hands wandered slowly behind and up her skirt, squeezing her soft bottom. Then he pulled her towards him and ran his nose up the length of her neck as he took in her scent. There was a long silence. So long it was as if time stood still. Then he pushed her away, gently.

"No," he said shaking his head. His eyes quickly zeroed in on two other lovelies hidden in the back.

"You and you, my dears; come, please..." His words were just as convincing as his beauty was.

In the few short seconds it took for them to close the distance, he was gesturing for the other girls to step aside and clear the way. And they did so, hesitantly but not before a few rolled eyes and dirty looks came their way. When the two chosen ones finally arrived within his reach, he leaned forward and ran his nose along the length of each girl's neck, one after the other. A few moments went by as he sat back against the couch glowing as if he'd just done a line of pure cocaine. His eyes glittered with hunger and smoldered with desire. The light in his eyes was like a vampire who had smelled and tasted blood.

"Yes," he whispered slow and lustfully. "Now that is pure Italian flesh my friends."

Robert's senses heightened and when his pulse changed, so did everyone else's. "You two will have the pleasure of my company," he told them. When he turned to his left, his eyes met Nathan and Tony's with euphoria; they could see the passion brewing inside him. "You two can have the rest," he said with conviction. "Have at it," he whispered.

It wasn't long before both girls were on their knees kissing and caressing his legs like two desperate tarts aching for him. They were alternating their motions on him, scattering their kisses as if it were some form of sacred worship...

While Robert was slipping deeper into his recollection, which played like a movie, he drifted into sleep.

In the other room down the hall was Beauty and her delicate nerves.

She tried desperately to sleep as she lay across her bed gazing into the fire, but it was useless. Having another man, besides her husband, inside her home had her on edge. She tossed and turned all night, occasionally checking her door to make sure it was locked. The last thing she needed was Robert wandering into her room, trying to get frisky with her. The constant sound of the raindrops against the window kept her from escape; from escaping the permanence her husband had left imprinted in her heart.

That was the first night.

CHAPTER 2 - Uncertainty

The next morning her eyes opened early. Blinded briefly by the bright rays of light shining through the window, she laid there for a moment still slightly dazed. Then her eyes swept around the room searching for him. She wandered innocently, but cautiously, down the hall in search of Robert Moses.

When she made it to the guest room, she pushed open the door and walked inside, but to her surprise, he wasn't in plain view. She focused her attention on the distinct sound of the blasting shower that was nearly drowned out by the TV he had left turned up.

She stood there a few moments admiring the lamp on the nightstand as if she were waiting for him, then she walked away.

As she made it to the door, something stopped her. Perhaps it was the curiosity lingering in the back of her mind. Subconsciously she was drawn toward him and, as though she were in a trance, her faint steps began toward the bathroom again where he was showering. She hid behind the door and hesitated a few seconds thinking how silly her actions were. Finally, she stuck her head out a few inches and peeked through the cracked door where she saw the hot, steamy, water running down his long frame through the glass shower door.

He didn't see her.

Her face softened as she stood there and watched him. It was the first time she noticed how handsome he truly was; so good looking she was offended by it, a little. *How dare he come around here flaunting his good looks at a lonely woman*, she thought, watching as he massaged soap between his legs.

Before she knew it, his massaging motion became more aggressive until he finally worked up a full erection. He went at it strong; stroking and pulling on himself, powerfully. Her eyes widened and immediately the rhythm of her breathing changed as her heart began pounding in her chest. Lost in the moment, she sighed then dropped her head for just a second.

And it was that motion that sent the vibration through the air that got his attention. He looked up quickly and caught a glimpse of her hair just as she pulled away. His confused expression quickly turned into something softer.

"Peeping, Lassie," he whispered through a smile, almost giggling. A few moments later, he walked into the guestroom with a long purple towel wrapped around his waist and to his surprise, there stood Beauty, waiting motionless, gazing at him with her hands behind her back.

He looks like he just stepped out of a painting, she thought, as he stood towering over her. His eyes were warm despite how much she hated to admit it. They were a mixture of gold and brown with a hint of burgundy; she'd never seen any like them before.

She tried to conceal the pleasure of Robert standing shirtless in front of her, but her eyes betrayed her. After all, he was the first man she'd seen in such a way since her husband. It had been ten long years since his passing and if she could have seen the way she stared in amazement, practically drooling, she would never admit to the feeling.

His eyes stared into her soul as they faced each other in silence. He could see the longing in her eyes as her hands appeared from behind her.

"Need a shirt?"

"As a matter of fact, I do. Mine…"

"I know," she interrupted. "Yours was soaked in blood so I took the liberty of finding one for you."

"Thank you."

"You're welcome," she said.

"So what type of woman keeps a man's 3X shirt lying around?" he asked as he slid the red flannel sleeves over his arms and shoulders. His question was sharp and precise; so sharp in fact that it nearly knocked the wind out of her.

"A widowed woman." she responded, tartly.

"I'm sorry." he whispered, eyes full of compassion.

"Well, don't be – that's life for you." When her eyes wandered out the window, she was reminded what a beautiful day it was. "Look, I'm gonna go for a walk – I'll see you when I get back – yeah."

"Of course, yeah. When you get back…"

Soon after, as she walked down the wooden porch steps outside,

Buddy blew past her, running off into the woods. You could see his power in the way his large body sliced through the air and the rumbling sound that came as his paws struck the ground.

"It's a beautiful day; perhaps, I could join you." he said, closing the door behind him.

She looked back over her shoulder to see Robert Moses standing on the porch waiting for her approval. His eyes were warm and full of life. She could see his attempt to disguise that cocky *I know I am handsome* smirk on his face. And he was handsome, she told herself as her face softened. Then she nodded gently.

And they began their walk into the woods watching Buddy sniff the scents from animals on trees up ahead. It was silent for several minutes as they admired the nature around them. The earthiness reminded Robert of some of the places he had traveled to in Europe.

"Funny how the sun shines so bright this morning but still it's so cold," he said smiling, blowing small clouds of fog out in front of them.

"That's my idea of a beautiful morning" she whispered seductively with both hands resting snug in her jean-jacket. It had a white wool liner around the collar that highlighted how classy she was. Then there were those tight, dark jeans she was wearing that clung to her like a second skin. Her dark hair glided in the light breeze that came and went.

Every now and then, her eyes peered briefly at him from behind her veil as she adjusted it. It was made of black suede and satin material and the fact that it was see through kept every part of her mystery alive by offering glimpses, but never a clear view, of her beauty.

22

They had strolled for twenty or more minutes when she stopped abruptly. Glancing at the ground beneath her, her mind flickered back to the images she'd seen there before. The red rose petals that covered the ground and her husband's warm lips on her tender naked skin. It was here, on this spot, he had made love to her countless times with the earthy scent of the forest permeating the air around them. Now, all that was left was the aroma and a mindful of memories.

"Are you OK? You seem saddened by this place?"

"I'm sorry."

"Don't be sorry."

"Thanks." She sighed as she came back to the present. "Just remembering happier times," she whispered, trying to disguise the sadness in her voice.

"It will get better for you Beauty; time heals all wounds, you know?"

"Thank you."

"You're welcome."

"I apologize if I was a bitch to you yesterday. It's just that my husband died in that house and, well, you're the first man that's come around here in ten years."

"Understood," he whispered, "I accept your apology."

She went hesitantly toward him and he pulled her closer, wrapped his arms around her in a lingering hug, and then let her go.

"See there. That's all you need; a nice warm hug," he said patting her on the back of her shoulders.

Maybe he's right, she thought. After all, he was the first man who'd given her so much as a lengthy stare in ten long years.

"You're healing pretty well. I've never seen anyone heal quite so fast. I mean, yesterday you could barely walk." She threw that statement out there as a fact but even more so to change the subject.

His eyes never left her. "Grief drives us to hunger for human touch," he murmured. "Something you've been deprived of for far too long."

She closed her eyes and took in the impact of his words. And then without warning, the sounds of rapid gunfire echoed through the woods violently as Robert pulled her to the ground, shielding her. It sounded like machine-guns firing as the bullets whistled relentlessly through the air. When she looked up, she saw the dirt flying up from the holes where the bullets were hitting the ground.

The next thing she saw made her heart skip a beat in her chest. On the lookout deck ahead, Buddy staggered back a few steps, crouched down, then leaped into the air, from one tree to another in an attempt to dodge the wild bullets that came his way.

"No!" she screamed as the shattered wood flew through the air around him. She could see Robert mouthing some words but the bullets screaming around them drowned him out. She wiggled free from under him a few moments later and began running toward the line of fire.

Robert followed soon after, perhaps to save her from herself. But all she could think about was saving Buddy and about what would happen if she didn't.

The more distance she closed between her and the tall tree Buddy hid in for his life, the more she noticed that the people launching the assault on him were hunters. She could see the camouflage they wore when her eyes rolled across them but strangely, they didn't see her. All of a sudden, the bullets stopped and arrows began shooting fiercely into the tree.

"Stop," she yelled loudly her voice echoing desperately through the woods.

Then the hunters stopped, but not before the sound of one last arrow sprung free and went slicing through the air. It traveled for what seemed like forever, her eyes following it with precision. A loud thud echoed as the tip of the arrow flew straight into the tree missing Buddy by inches. It vibrated for a moment from the force of the impact.

Her expression softened briefly before outrage and disbelief marked it. "Have you people lost your mind?" She yelled furiously stepping toward them.

"That's a dangerous looking animal there," one of the men blurted, "and we're licensed hunters miss, uhh…"

"But this is private property," She interrupted. "That means you can't be on it and that animal belongs to me."

The tone of her voice told them she meant business. The hunters stood there dumbfounded thinking of what to do next while Beauty's eyes met Buddy's behind the obscurity of the swaying trees.

She could see the terror in his eyes but also the relief to see her standing there. When she returned her attention to where the men were standing, she noticed Robert standing by her side. She also noticed the impact his presence had on the hunters. They were intimidated and their body language reeked of fear.

"Alright, gentlemen. This is how it's gonna go," she said firmly. "You will tell no one what you saw here. You will vacate my property and I won't report you for trespassing."

"Did the lady not make herself clear?" Robert asked devilishly as the men hesitated. His strong accent had a way of strategically getting across how serious he was, not to mention the nine millimeter he carried in his waistband. His eyes signaled how capable of evil he was as they flickered with a thirst for altercation.

"We understand just fine," one of the older men blurted, as he led the others away.

After a few seconds, her eyes met Robert's and then Buddy's.

"Come here, boy," she called clicking her mouth as he hesitantly came down from the tree and into her arms. "It's okay," she murmured, kissing him and running her hands over his lean coat checking him for wounds. A wave of relief came over her and she exhaled for the first time since hearing the gunfire.

Robert watched them reunite for several moments, admiring the simplicity of what made her happy. Then they headed back to the lake house.

CHAPTER 3 – On a Human Level

It was several hours later when the sound of her voice calling him from down the hall made his eyes light up. He went toward it, thinking of how crazy a day it had been, wondering what could happen next. Then he saw her beautiful slim frame go across the hallway enthusiastically as if she were excited about something. She peeked around the corner playfully, just as he walked into the living room. Then, she flashed a warm smile and gestured for him to follow her out onto the balcony. Closing the door behind him, his face softened when he saw the steam ascending from the two fresh cups of coffee on the table. He closed his eyes and inhaled deeply.

"I never would have guessed you were a Taster's Choice kind of gal," he whispered, exhaling with a warm smile on his face.

His sense of smell is very keen, she thought as she stood beside him, watching the snowflakes falling icily from the dark sky.

"Quite unbelievable, you think. This morning was full of sunshine and now it's snowing."

His accent made her giggle. She had always been fond of British accents but to hear that from a black guy really tickled her.

"Why are you laughing at me?" he asked her sarcastically.

All she could do was shake her head and smile as she handed him his cup of coffee.

When she faced him, he paid more attention to her frame. His eyes wandered up her long, slender, legs admiring the way her white jeans hugged every curve. He flashed his eyes at the black turtleneck she wore, his eyes running over her breasts carefully and then he turned away. He thought about how pert and firm they were before trying to snap himself out of it.

"I owe you an apology, Robert," she said softly after taking a sip of coffee. The fog from the cold air lingered there a moment after her words. Her narrowed eyes darted into his with a sparkle as a cold breeze blew her dark hair away from her face.

"I've been rude to you since you got here and still you had my back earlier; thank you," she whispered blinking.

The emotion in her voice resonated with him as he took a step closer to her, placing his hands on the ledge next to hers.

"With great pleasure I accept your apology. Though, I must say, a second apology isn't necessary. Not even the first," he added. "It was me who came disrupting a woman trying to live a life of simplicity."

There was a brief silence and the quietness of the woods became more apparent. His words had a way of penetrating her; she could sense the sincerity in them when he spoke.

"I'm really sorry to hear about your husband. How did he die – might I ask?"

Her head dropped for a moment, hesitating as he awaited her response. Her facial expression told him how painful the subject was; he could see the despair growing in her eyes.

"Cancer," she said softly. Her voice was just a whisper when the tears on her saturated eyelids ran slowly down the side of her face. She tipped her head slightly and smiled halfheartedly trying to push away the memories, and perhaps the loneliness, that lingered in her heart. There was a signal between them that had begun in that moment. Her eyes were full of emotion and so were his; the look in them told her she was beautiful. She could see the light in his gold-brown eyes as they met hers with a deep stare.

Then, he put his fingertips to her cheek and wiped away her tears. "Things will change for you, you know..."

His voice was so persuasive that it was as if he desensitized her right there. Her cheeks burned from the cold but it wasn't the cold that made her weak. Before she knew it, he kissed her on the cheek and then headed off the porch into the forest.

He winked and told her to follow him. She suppressed a smile still stunned by what was happening. But, as he walked further away, both curiosity and adrenaline took over and she followed after him.

When she breached the boundary that separated the lake house from the forest, she discovered the snow on the ground was deeper the further out she went. Beauty called out his name a few times before she realized he was hiding from her. Her eyes swept over the forest hoping to catch a glimpse of him. It was a quiet and eerily beautiful night, she thought as her eyes continued wandering.

A few short seconds later, he appeared from behind a tree. But not before the snowball he threw at her sent Beauty to the ground landing on her backside.

They broke into laughter and then he came and lay down next to her. She was a little embarrassed but his calm reassuring presence soon took that away.

"You're not opposed to a little fun?" he asked gently.

All Beauty could do was shake her head and laugh as she felt a part of herself suspended in time gazing up at the stars with him.

They stayed there for a while and talked.

He told her a little about how he had come from England when he was eighteen and briefly attended college in Nevada. "But, college wasn't for me," he said shrugging his shoulders as a shooting star went blazing across the sky. The discontent in his voice was poorly disguised; she could tell there was more he wasn't telling her.

When Beauty asked him what he meant, he shied away intentionally and continued, "We must respect the boundaries of destiny," he said cleverly. His golden-brown eyes twinkled as he spoke and the effect his accent had on his words only left her more mystified.

When they arrived back at the lake house, they were both shivering from the cold. She went into the living room and started the fireplace. The sound of the flame igniting, the warmth, and the crackling of wood immediately gave her a sense of release. When she closed her eyes for a brief moment, she could feel his masculine presence behind her.

He called her name and she pretended not to hear him as she struggled to keep her knees from buckling.

"Let's get you out of these wet clothes," he said slow and seductively.

As she realized what he was saying, her heart began skipping beats in her chest.

When Beauty finally faced him, she could see the hunger in his eyes and perhaps he could see the longing in hers.

His eyes lit up like a vampire ready to quench his thirst and Beauty sensed that he could somehow feel how hard her heart was pounding.

He stared at her for a moment with that deep stare of his; the more he did, the more she could feel her desire aching inside. Finally, he came closer; interlocking his fingers with hers, then he kissed her deeply.

It was then she let herself go and allowed all of the pent-up passion to take over...

He ran his nose up the length of her neck inhaling her beautiful, distinctive feminine scent.

Breathe, she reminded herself while his strong hands helped her out of her clothes, placing tender kisses around her shoulders.

Now, completely naked, she shook free her dark hair that hung beautifully down her back.

Then it was her turn. She ran her hands over his growing manhood before removing his jeans, boxers and shirt.

Robert pulled Beauty to her knees in front of the fireplace and put his warm lips on her tender, naked skin. He maneuvered his lips down her shoulders kissing her gently while his hands wandered down her backside.

Before she knew it, he was sucking on her breasts like candy while his hands went over the heat of her flesh. He could smell the lust hidden between her crevices as he squeezed her soft bottom and ran his hot tongue up the length of her neck. Her deep breathing brought more attention to just how tantalizing it was. The more excited he became, the tighter his grip became around her.

Suddenly, she pulled away from him and licked her lips suggestively before leaning forward and taking him into her warm mouth.

The sound of the wood burning in the fireplace only heightened the sense of things. She handled him with finesse as if she were polishing brass. He watched her for a moment before pushing her away.

"Bend over," he ordered as he smacked her across the backside. The sound of it echoed through the air. Then, mounting her from behind, he held a fistful of her dark hair in his hand as he drove himself into her pink heaven. Harder and harder he went, skin against skin, as he rode her. She swung her hips back to meet his thrusts, which weakened her with every stride. They continued for twenty minutes before simultaneously releasing themselves in an explosion of ecstasy.

CHAPTER 4 – Turbulence 1

The next morning came quickly. Her eyes opened to the sound of Buddy growling in the distance. It was a frustrated growl she thought, and then she remembered that she had locked him in his room the night before. She ran her hands through her dark hair, wandered down the hallway in a long T-shirt, and set him free.

Then, she heard a knock at the front door. Her first thought was somehow Robert had been locked out of the lake house, but quickly dismissed that idea when she heard the sound of the blasting shower down the other hall.

It was an awkward realization. *People don't usually come around here,* she thought, and definitely not so early in the morning. She peeked through the curtain briefly then opened the door to see two men standing on the porch.

Two white men. One was heavy set; the other was tall and slim with a thick moustache. They both wore cowboy hats, Wrangler shirts and fancy, custom cowboy boots. She could see their horses standing in the distance. It was the Sheriff's badge that she noticed on the slim-man's shirt that made her nervous.

"Good morning, ma'am, we're really sorry to bother you," he said tipping his hat at her.

Her next thought was those damn hunters had reported Buddy to the authorities after all and they were here to take him away.

"Yes ma'am. We're out just canvassing the area and we wanted to let you know there was a prison escape a few days ago."

When she heard that, she sighed with relief and smiled, projecting her beauty. Thank God she thought.

"You wouldn't have seen this man have you?" the heavier man blurted pulling a paper from his coat and showing it to her.

Her eyes moved over the photo and what she saw sent chills up her spine. It was a mug shot of Robert Moses staring back at her. Her thoughts flew back to his strange arrival earlier in the week as she tried to disguise the repressed fury in her eyes.

"You look lost in thought ma'am," he said with a smile.

"No, I'm sorry. I was just thinking of how careful we have to be these days. I mean, this man doesn't even look like a criminal."

"Well, he is," he said in a serious tone. "And if you encounter him in any way, give us a call," he said handing her a business card.

When they began walking down the wooden porch steps, she couldn't help herself. "What did he do, Sheriff?" she asked curiously and desperately at the same time.

"Let's just say we've got a murder on our hands," he said climbing on his horse and heading back into the forest.

There was silence as she thought about what he had said.

When she went back inside, she locked the door behind her and stood there for a moment.

Breathe, she told herself as her head dropped for a second thinking of how stupid she'd been. When she looked up, she saw him there, standing in front of her. Her eyes were full of betrayal. He had overheard everything and he knew she was on to him. Her eyes scorched with irritation as she shook her head in disbelief.

"I guess that's it," he whispered, softly.

"You guess that's it?" she repeated, mocking him. "You came into my house, I saved your life, you lied to me, made love to me, used me – and you guess that's it? You're an asshole, Robert!"

When she said that, his eyes closed a moment as the pain from her words stung him.

"Perhaps you're right. Maybe I am a bit of an asshole but I never used you, Beauty." His body language made it clear how traitorous he felt. "For what it's worth, Beauty, I withheld this certain thing from you because I didn't want to see the look you have on your face now."

After that, she sunk to the floor with tears of disappointment flooding her eyes.

His expression reflected the same as he sat down beside her.

"I have the worst luck in the world." She said gently. "I fall in love with the man of my dreams and he dies to cancer. Then, for ten years I live alone – here, struggling to put the pieces back together. And just when I think I might have a chance at finding love again, I discover that you're a fugitive. Now you tell me, is that not the worst luck, Robert?"

"I'm so sorry Beauty, I…"

"No," she interrupted putting her finger to his mouth. "It gets worse," she said. "About a week before you arrived, I found out that I have Stage 4 – Leukemia. I'm dying, Robert."

After those words, he turned away in disbelief with his mouth hung open. Then, he reached over and interlocked his fingers with hers. The moment was serious.

"How many people escaped with you from prison," she asked innocently taking his attention away from the bad news she had just given him.

His expression lightened briefly as he realized how fascinated by it she seemed.

"Just one other; he died, I survived…if you call this surviving."

The next thing they heard was a man's voice booming through a bullhorn outside.

Beauty quickly sprung to her feet and peeked out the curtain. It was the Sheriff and his crony. They had returned.

"Robert Moses, we know you're in there. Why don't you come out so nobody gets hurt?"

His heart kicked up a notch and so did hers when he peeked out the curtain and tried to think what to do next.

"Robert Moses you've got two minutes to come out with your hands up, or we're comin' in there!"

His eyes met Beauty's with uncertainty and sadness; it was as if he wanted her opinion of what she thought he should do. They stared at each other for several seconds; those seconds seem like forever. She kissed him one last time before she pulled away.

"Robert, hurry; go in the master bedroom and lift up the Persian rug. There's a panel underneath it, which unlocks the door leading to a tunnel underground. Follow that tunnel for a mile until you see a red door. On the other side, will be a horse and a couple days worth of food. They won't catch you if you go now," she reluctantly whispered.

He scrambled for a moment taking in the genius of what she'd said and, without warning, he disappeared but not before declaring he would see her again.

"I will come for you, my lady."

It was the last thing she heard as he took off through the house...

A few moments later, the sound of his shoes hitting the pavement in the underground tunnel gave him a brief sense of relief. His eyes wandered carefully as he sprinted down the dimly lit tunnel ahead.

He could hear himself panting as he saw haystacks that stretched along both of the walls. *It's her emergency stash*, he thought, as he kept moving.

Finally, he reached the red door and walked through it without hesitation. On the other side was freedom. The fresh air was the first sign that he had reached the end of the tunnel and he took a deep breath. Then, there on his left, stood a beautiful grey horse. He could tell he was a strong horse from the way his muscles flirted underneath his smooth, shiny skin.

"Here, boy," he said clicking his tongue gently. Immediately this beautiful creature came over to him. His hand went over his skin when their eyes met. "Now I need you to be a good boy and take me far away. Okay?" Robert's heart was still throbbing in his chest and his adrenaline was pumping like crazy. The mission was clear; he had to get out of there.

It only took him a few minutes to saddle up with a few days provisions and take off at a dead run. He rode for hours up the rugged terrain and into the mountains before sliding off his horse and resting for a while.

There he rested under the camouflage of massive trees hand feeding some apples to his new friend.

"And what shall I call you, friend," he whispered searching for a name. It was then, for the first time, that his eyes stumbled upon the realization that his new friend was female. "Now, how about that? I think I'll call you Beauty," he said with a giggle. He stayed there for a while and before he knew it, the darkness of night settled in.

When he opened his eyes, he blinked them a few times, still dazed by the light that met them. Then he saw two men standing over him; one kicking at his foot and the other spitting tobacco juice arrogantly in the dirt beside him.

"You alive, boy?" he asked as he dumped a pail of water on Robert Moses' face.

"Yeah, he's alive, Sheriff." Said the deputy.

Then the Sheriff lit a cigarette, pulled on it a few times and blew smoke into the air.

The smell of the smoke in his nostrils immediately took his mind back to all of the tobacco he'd smelled in prison.

"Now, you know just about all of Texas is looking for you, Robert? It took those damn bloodhounds forever to sniff you out. We'd lost your scent for a while there but they picked it back up." He paused for a moment then, pulled on his cigarette again.

All Robert could think about was how mad at himself he was for letting exhaustion get the best of him; and for falling asleep in the Texas woods so close to freedom. He laid motionless on his back trying to gain his wits about himself. His disappointed face even drew sympathy from the Sheriff.

After all, Robert Moses wasn't just a prison escapee, he was a world renowned celebrity famous for the twenty-odd books he'd authored. He had made millions in prison and even more since the word of his escape. Everyone knew that about him – except Beauty and perhaps that was one of the reasons he was drawn to her.

"So, what now?" he asked reluctantly, as his eyes stared into the soul of the Sheriff.

The Sheriff turned away and sighed with a halfhearted crooked smile on his face. "Oh, I don't know, Robert. I was hoping you could tell me that; being a rich man and all."

A flicker of hope shot through his eyes for the first time as he stood to attention. "Are we negotiating, Sheriff?"

"Maybe," he said pulling something out of his leather coat and handing it to him. "You know my twenty-three-year-old daughter has read all of your books. She admires you; would you mind signing one for her?"

When their eyes met, they stared at each other with a wicked smile in light of the awkward circumstances. *Imagine that,* he thought while gripping the pen and signing the book.

"A loyal fan, have we? You must tell your daughter how refreshing I find that. I am concocting something extra special for my fans next year. Well, that was a piece of cake, Sheriff. Now, where were we?"

"We're at the point where I capture and take you back to where you belong; prison!" he blurted, "And for a long time."

Robert's reaction was strange as the realization that he'd just been manipulated settled in.

"I know that wasn't a nice thing to do but…" He paused for a moment and took a swig of whiskey from his silver flask. "As much as I'd like to see you ride that horse off into the sunset, for, let's say, five hundred grand. The truth is, there're too many people out here looking for you and that's a risk I'm not willing to take. Besides, bringing you in will give me a raise and bring the Police Department a shit load of good publicity. Hell, I wanna be famous, too."

There was a long silence. Then, his partner came closer. "So," he said, taking a deep breath. "Robert Moses you are under arrest for felony escape from the Texas Department of Corrections."

When the Sheriff said that, everything faded. All he remembered was the sound of the handcuffs clicking and tightening around his wrists before he was transported back to prison...

CHAPTER 5 – Lion's Den

Three hours later, his greeting back on the prison grounds was like a hero's welcome from the inmates. Even a few of the guards secretly admired what he did. Here was a man who always seemed to finesse himself out of situations despite the circumstances. Moreover, he vowed he would do it again.

The last thing he'd said to Beauty before he left was, "I will come for you my lady." He replayed that image in his mind over and over and couldn't seem to shake free from the awful thought of her illness. She deserved better and she would get it if he had anything to say about it.

Upon his arrival, he was taken to an observation cell in the infirmary. It was a place where he could be watched and where nurses could check him for any injuries he may have suffered. For the next hour or more, people entered and exited his cell. Then it went quiet and the lights dimmed down a bit.

Soon he heard a sound and saw an inmate named Porter mopping down the hallway towards him. Porter stopped mopping when he realized Robert was staring at him.

Though people had become familiar with Robert, the novelty had never worn off; they were still as star struck by him as the day he arrived there fifteen years ago.

"I'm sorry they caught you," he said with disappointment, "We were all cheering for you in here."

Robert nodded his understanding and tried to focus. "Listen, I need a cell phone as soon as possible," he whispered, "Do you think you can handle that?"

There was silence as he stared deep into the eyes of the man to whom he had directed his request. Being face-to-face with Robert was like being in the presence of a general or a prophet. When he spoke, he spoke with conviction. His requests were more like giving orders than asking for a favor; that was the power of this man. And so it was arranged for the next day.

The next day came and went, then another day passed. His disappointed expression became more noticeable when he was moved from one part of the institution to another. He was placed back in general population, only this time in a more secure housing unit.

But to him, it didn't matter where they took him; he was who he was. When he walked back through the gate, he heard screams, whistling, and hurrahing from inmates on the prison yard. Escorted by officers with video cameras, his return to prison gained a lot of publicity on all of the local news stations and even a few national stations.

He smiled, acknowledging with a nod and a wave of his hand the respect they gave him. But anyone who knew him could tell by his facial expression that he wasn't content by any stretch of the imagination. That look said he'd seen it all before.

Several hours drifted by as he sat with his eyes sweeping across his new home. It was strangely quiet he thought. And then, a white envelope slid underneath the door followed by a flat, palm-sized, black cell phone.

A moment later he sprung to his feet glancing out the glass window of his cell to meet the eyes of a young-looking white male officer staring back at him.

He winked and walked away but not before Robert mouthed the words "Thank you." He turned the envelope over and saw her name in script written across the top left corner. Inside was a message that read:

Dear Robert,

Our short time together is something I will treasure forever. You made me smile when I thought I didn't have any smiles left. You are a good man. Thank you.

The day after your departure I collapsed suddenly and was air-lifted to the hospital. I began chemotherapy today, which has left me weak but I am still able to envision your handsome face.

I suspect I may be in love with you, Robert.

Write Soon,
Beauty

∞

Dear Beauty,

I don't believe I've ever read a letter that touched me as deeply as yours has. Thank you for your time. Maybe I deserve it; maybe I don't. I'm still trying to figure that part out. What I do know is that you are deserving Beauty; deserving of better than what's been placed upon you. And I will do whatever I must do to ensure that your last moments aren't spent alone. It can be done, Beauty. It will be done...

Love,
Robert

PS. I suspect that I'm in love with you too...

One week later, his eyes drifted out the window ten minutes after he awakened. He watched as a blonde female officer flirted with one of the inmates. That was normal around there, women being so taken aback by the attention from caged cons. However, that wasn't what surprised Robert; it was who the pretty blonde was flirting with; Mr. Bobby Jones.

Bobby was infamous throughout the prison system but it wasn't for being a gentleman and a scholar. He had multiple rapes, the ones he was in prison for, and several others he'd picked up while in prison (on inmates). Robert never understood how he kept getting released - especially after so many offenses - time after time.

Perhaps the young lady wonders the same, he thought then dismissed the thought, rationalizing that she probably wouldn't be speaking to him if she knew who he was.

Prison was funny like that. It wasn't like in the movies where it was all terror, horror and screaming. What a lot of people forget is that these are real people with real feelings and everyone's body language tells a story. Some inmates were sorry for what they did; some were not. *It is the nature of the beast,* he thought to himself.

One thing was for certain, fear could be smelled in the air from a mile away and a lot of people thrived on that; especially Bobby Jones. That was how he picked his victims, mostly youngsters; first time offenders who were new in prison without a clue of how things work in a place like that. Everyone feared Bobby; he stood six feet ten inches and weighed 300lbs – solid muscle.

Everyone feared him - except Robert, that is. Bobby knew Robert was physically strong and a masterful thinker and it always made him leery of Robert. Robert recalled telling him years ago that if he ever tried anything funny with anyone he had ever thrown a brotherly arm around he would destroy him himself.

Robert took a seat next to him a few days later on the prison yard. They sat in the bleachers watching as some of the guys played baseball.

"Such a beautiful, lovely day Bobby, huh?"

"Yes it is," he returned in his deep voice.

"You know, I couldn't help but notice the way that gal swooned at you the other day."

"You saw that too, huh? What can I say, I'm irresistible man."

Robert's eyes lit up with a twinkle he got when he was enthused about something.

"Personally I thought I was mistaken at first glance. Until she…"

"Until she what?" Bobby asked excitedly.

Robert hesitated a moment trying to suppress a faint smile. "Until she inquired about you; that was all the confirmation I needed," he added.

"Is that right? Well, what did she say?"

There was another silence as, his eyes darted into Bobby's contemplatively.

"She fancies you, Bobby," he said in his sharp accent. "But those weren't her words of course. If my recollection is correct, she said to meet her tomorrow night in her office. Eleven P.M. sharp, if you can handle her," he added.

Bobby began nodding and rubbing his hands together cleverly, as he processed what Robert told him.

"And so, I'll go along and be your lookout Bobby; make sure you don't get caught, yeah."

"I owe you one, Robert. I knew there was always something I liked about you."

They shook hands and parted ways.

Later that night, another envelope came sliding under the door. It was from Beauty.

Dear Robert,

I received your letter a week ago and I have no words to describe how happy it made me. The chemo has made me very weak; I'm practically bedridden. But, there are moments when I get a burst of energy, mostly when I think about you.

My hair is thinning so rapidly that I just keep a scarf over it now. I can't believe how fast all this is happening. I know death awaits me Robert but I will fight for as long as I can. I know you're up to something in there and I just want you to know, I'm pulling for you baby... :-)

Love,
Beauty

After reading the letter, he closed his eyes a moment; tears spilling over his eyelids as the pain of her words sunk in. Prison didn't matter in this case, what mattered was saving Beauty or at least making sure she didn't die alone. She deserved better, he kept telling himself.

Sitting in his little blue chair with his cup of coffee steaming in his hand he daydreamed of their picnic in the forest; the thought was bittersweet. He snapped out of it, climbed onto the bed, and exhaled deeply. Once he was down, the exhaustion settled on him like a weight as he lay there in the silence.

The next day came and began moving like a dust storm fueled by the pressure of the wind. Before he knew it, it was nightfall; 10:55 pm. He remembered when he glanced at his watch that he had an appointment with Bobby.

He met Bobby's eyes and gave him a nod of approval with a restrained smile. There were four inmates standing in the day room when a woman's voice came over the intercom and told them to return to their cells. There was a brief hesitation as they tried to soak up their last few minutes of freedom and then it went silent... The only two people out of their cells were Robert and Bobby Jones.

When the lights dimmed it added a sense of how wrong all of this was Robert thought as he gestured with his hand for Bobby to go ahead. "I'll look out for you," he whispered with a smirk on his face, "Go," he said winking at him.

And it was the encouragement that gave Bobby the courage he needed as he stalked off and walked through the door.

Her back was towards Bobby. He closed the blinds just before the sound of the door shutting startled her. When she turned around and faced him, she smiled but her smile and his smile were not the same as before.

"Hey Bobby, you scared the shit out of me – Whoa," she said glancing at her watch and looking at him with suspicion. "You're supposed to be locked down already. Can I help you with something?" she asked.

The look in his eyes changed and the expression on his face was pure evil. He stood in front of the door for several moments, staring at her. The sudden speed of his assault came when he snatched her in his arms and threw her halfway across the room. She landed face down on the floor with a viciousness that shook her to the core. Her radio slid out a few feet away from her but not before she was able to press the panic button. Some sick-twisted part of Bobby's mind thought that she was role-playing. He turned her over, pinned her wrists down on the floor, and yanked at her pants.

"No!" she screamed.

And it was the scream that sent Robert bursting into the room. He grabbed the fire extinguisher from the wall and hit Bobby in the back of the head with it knocking him out cold. The sound of the metal rung like a bell when it hit him. Suddenly the corrections officers were there but the woman was still shaking frantically.

Bobby was hauled off on a stretcher and Robert in handcuffs.

"Bastard tried to rape me," she said, trying to catch her breath as the sirens and alarms whooping in the distance stopped abruptly.

"Are you OK?"

"Yeah, yeah, I'm OK," she told one of the officers nearby.

"After you finish getting checked out by medical, the lieutenant will want to see you to give a statement about what happened here."

She nodded in agreement still freaked out by the incident.

The next night came swiftly, it seemed. Robert was in the hole, a dark isolated cell by himself waiting to see what would happen next. His thoughts went over the possible outcomes. He knew what mattered most would be the statement the woman gave and he needed it to be an honest one. In fact, he depended on her honesty like the heartbeat in his chest. He also reminded himself that this was still prison and that anything could happen. He closed his eyes and thought for a moment.

When they opened he saw the woman's face peering through the window then the cell door opened and she stepped into the cell.

His eyes met hers wonderingly as she came closer, then stopped in front of him. The first thing he noticed was her warm eyes; it was those eyes that assured him everything would be okay.

"Are you alright, Miss Price?" he whispered quietly, reading her name off the nametag sewn into her uniform.

"I'm alright, thanks to you," she murmured softly. She smiled and he smiled back with that same warm-hearted smile.

"No one deserves what he tried to do to you, I'm just glad I could help."

Then, without warning, a man in a black suit walked in behind her. His face looked familiar Robert thought and then, it hit him – hard. It was the warden. But what was he doing here?

"Good morning Robert," he blurted with enthusiasm. "I just wanted to come down and shake the hand of the man that saved my daughter's life."

It was a stunning realization, he thought. "You know, I was reviewing your file Robert and uhh -" he hesitated a moment as if he were trying to find the right words to say. "Taking into account the fifteen years you've already served, I believe you would be a great candidate for a pardon."

Hearing those words took his breath away and sent chills up his spine.

"I'll email the governor and it should be no problem getting both his signature and you out of here by this time tomorrow night. If that's okay with you, Robert Moses?"

Robert smiled at his sarcasm then nodded and said, "I'd be very delighted; how could I ever repay you?"

There was a brief silence as his eyes met Robert's and then his daughter's. "You already have," he said with a smile, grabbing his daughter's hand and exiting the cell.

Robert sighed a deep sigh of relief. His plan had worked; he would see

Beauty again...

CHAPTER 6 – Getting There

Before he knew it, his day had arrived. The thick fog that lingered between the trees muffled the sound of his horse maneuvering through the woods, over the wet branches and rough terrain.

 He rode for an hour and stopped in front of the lake house. He sat there for a moment like a horseman from another time draped in a black-hooded robe that covered his head and stopped just short of his brown alligator boots. The sound of his horse neighing in relief was the last thing he heard as he stepped through the lake house door...

It was as if the dimension of time changed as his eyes wandered through each room desperately trying to find her. Down the hall, he met Buddy standing motionless staring back at him. The sadness in his eyes told Robert something was wrong and then he led him into the bedroom where she was lying on the bed – barely clinging to life.

His eyes watered with tears from what he saw. She looked as if she had aged 30 years from the last time he saw her just a few weeks before. The thought of seeing her that way broke his heart.

"I came for you, my lady," he whispered.

At the sound of his voice she turned her head a little and a grim smile came to her face. Her eyes lit up with the last bit of life she had left in her.

Seeing her weakened condition hit him hard. It made him realize how powerful cancer was and how it could rapidly slip out of control.

She stared at him in silence – thinking how Robert's presence assured her that she would die an honorable death; she wouldn't die alone she thought as she gestured for him to sit on the bed next to her.

"Read me something from the book you're writing," she whispered faintly.

"Of course, my lady," he said returning a halfhearted smile while unrolling the manuscript from his robe. He adjusted the papers in his hand and wrapped his arm around her with the other. He smiled gently restraining a smile of sadness and began reading.

"Persuasion," he read. *"Such a powerful, underestimated word. A word that haunted him since the first day he set foot in a courtroom fifteen years ago. He had always been a fan of magic and how the genius of one's mind could create an optical illusion – leaving onlookers mystified right before their very own eyes. The thought of it fueled his ego, especially since Joshua dabbled in a little magic of his own. But, he didn't call it that and he prided himself on his authenticity. Doubt me not, what Joshua did was not an illusion, it was real – very real. Pure, laser light – verbal incision at a level, it was almost as if he could compel you and place thoughts right into your mind."*

He paused for a moment. Then his eyes wandered down to Beautys. He could see her listening to him but he could also see her fading slowly into the next life.

"I don't want to die, Robert," the sound of her weak voice murmured. And it was those words that spoke to his soul.

"You don't have to my lady. I can save you." There was a brief silence as his eyes held still into hers. "I'm – Immortal my lady, I'm a vampire, Beauty. But if I do this, my love, you must know there is no turning back." His passionate eyes locked with hers hoping that she understood the depth of what he said. "It will mean no more aging Love, you too will be Immortal forever," he whispered.

"Don't let me die," was the last thing she said before her eyes rolled up into the back of her head.

The veins beneath his eyes pulsated under his skin, as his fangs emerged completely. Then, his eyes blackened just before he sunk his fangs deep into her neck. He held her still a moment while the healing within him raced through her bloodstream. Then he waited, hoping he had caught her before she had left this planet.

Several moments passed before he began to see her transition from the old woman she'd become back to her youthful appearance before his very eyes. *It worked,* he thought as he closed his eyes and sighed in relief.

Then, her baffled screams cut through the air like, hot steam on a cold day.

"Beauty, it's OK. It's OK, my love," he repeated wrapping his arms around her. "You're alright now." His thick accent and dreamy eyes helped her to come back.

"Immortal beloved," he whispered slowly. "I have something I have to say and you need to hear it once. If anyone finds out who we are, it will be bad. You know that, right?"

"Yes," she said with reluctance still trying to make sense of what had happened. Her eyes wandered the room then returned to his.

"How did you do that, Robert? You saved me, I can't believe …"

"Hush now, my lady," he interrupted putting his finger to her lips. "There are so many things you must know; so much, you must learn my love."

"I can hear Robert, I can hear. Hear things in the forest I never heard before."

He smiled gently and then giggled for a moment at how fascinated she seemed by all this.

"Yes, all of your senses are heightened now. The ability to hear, see and feel like you've never done before love. I can teach you how to control all of these senses but there's nothing like having a little fun," he said flashing through the house in a flicker; disappearing in the blink of an eye. The candles went out suddenly and the smoke from them lingered in the air.

"Beauty," his voice called out echoing slowly through the lake house.

A soft, gentle smile covered her face amazed at the game he was playing with her. She stood motionless for a moment trying to eavesdrop and get a sense for where he was when all of a sudden she felt his swift animal-like movements breaking the air around her. But, her glimpses weren't enough to catch him. Her eyes wandered suspiciously for a moment with that beautiful smile when she felt a warm draft of air blowing her negligee over thighs then undoing her bra. She couldn't see him but she could feel him.

His gentle touch explored the heaven of her crevices. The sensation was incredible she thought as she closed her eyes and let him have his way.

He ran his fingers along her feminine core sending a tingling sensation throughout her body. Then, he planted a passionate, deep kiss against her lips.

When her eyes opened, there he stood, barely visible at first. His ghost-like image was transforming back to something more human right before her eyes.

"Everything smooth over here," he said with a smile as the dark night lit by the moon peered through on their faces.

"How did you become so clever?"

"You mean cunning, my lady."

"Yes. I tried to listen to find where you might be – but nothing. What's up with that?"

"Oh, don't be too hard on yourself, love; all things come in time."

"I know... But tell me why. Why couldn't I find you?"

His eyes flashed at her then wandered out the window and then returned. "You weren't fully focused; you weren't listening with all your senses. Come." he said gesturing with a nod to follow him outside.

They stood on the dark porch and gazed out into the forest.

"I'll turn on the porch light, Robert; it's dark out here."

"No – Shh," he whispered grabbing her hand and pulling her back. "It's better this way. Now try to focus – listen, Beauty. Listen."

She stood motionless for a moment and her expression was unreadable.

"I can't, Robert; I just -"

"Listen, my love … with all your heart," he said gently. His voice was so persuasive.

She took a deep breath and went into a stillness. Several seconds later, tangled chaos flooded her ears as the sound of the water flowing off the rocks upstream emerged.

"I can hear, I can hear," she said like a silly, giddy girl.

He saw the change in her expression and it made him warm and her too. Witnessing her taking in a new fragment of her new ability told him that progress had been made.

"Well," he said taking a deep breath. "Now on to something more complicated; and for this, I do apologize my lady but I must continue." Seriousness came over him.

Her mind thought of what in the world he might say.

"What if I told you that Buddy must be turned tonight?" he asked.

Her frowned expression quickly filled with uncertainty. "Well, I don't know. Why – I mean?"

"It's his scent, my lady," he interrupted sharply. "I can smell him – They can smell him which means they're looking for us..."

"Who?" her desperate voice blurted as she grabbed his wrist gently.

"Vampire hunters – human hunters, witches and your human scents all over him. They're near NOW and it'll be best if we leave tomorrow."

"But I've lived here forever, Robert; where do you think we're supposed to go?"

"Let's just say my home away from home and let it be a surprise."

Her face softened and so did his. He could see a glimmer of trust building in her eyes but still a hint of hesitation.

"So what about Buddy? If I do this, how will it affect him?" She asked.

Robert's eyes wandered away for a moment scanning the forest but then returned.

"Well, he'll be stronger and more vicious; have heightened senses, and the only thing that can claim his life is a stake to the heart. How does that sound?"

"Those are the pros, how about the cons?"

"My love," he said with a hint of frustration, "Let's just focus on the pros." There was a brief silence and he could see her thinking, debating with herself. "I know how much you love Buddy and I want him around just as much as you do, but I can assure if you don't do this – he won't be..."

The impact of his blunt words undid her.

A few moments later, he planted a kiss against her cheek and squeezed her hand gently. "Don't worry, I'm here with you. I'll walk you through it," he whispered in her ear before whistling and calling Buddy's name.

Beauty repeated a few more times afterwards when finally he pushed through the half-opened door onto the porch.

She knelt down and began petting him. Robert did the same while he observed her sad eyes sweep over his smooth face sharing her last moments with him before he became something different. Then her head dropped down a little before her eyes met with his.

"Robert, I don't know if I can do this. I feel like I'm doing something wrong."

"Of course you can do it, my lady. You must do it."

"Well, can you help me a little?"

He nodded hesitantly with his arms crossed firmly, "I can – but there's something you need to do first."

"What?"

"Get mad," he stated sharply as his swift hand went smacking her across the face. She hesitated a moment closing her eyes as she took in the impact of the sting. When they opened, they were black – all black. Her veins pulsated beneath her skin and the darkness in her eyes illuminated with pure evil. Then he moved a little closer, his eyes never leaving hers.

"Now that I've got your attention, I want you to sink your teeth into his neck – NOW!" She turned and drove her fangs into him while Robert held him still.

"Alright, my lady; that's enough."

"That's enough," he repeated, pulling her away from him.

Finally, she released her grip sending Buddy falling on the wooden porch floor, wailing desperately. Beauty staggered back a few steps and fell on her backside. She wiped some of the blood from her mouth watching in horror as the reality of what she'd done played out before her. The baffled screams of her loyal friend whistled through the cold air, shattering her each time he cried out.

"Robert – something's wrong."

"No," he interrupted sharply, "He's fine. Just give him a moment – yeah."

Against her better judgment, she stopped herself from aiding him. Perhaps, it was Robert's persuasive voice. After all, he had saved her life. Who was she to question him?

Several moments later, Buddy's cries faded away, but he was still breathing. The contractions in his stomach ceased, offering a sense of relief, as he seemed to regain control over his breathing. Then, as they watched, the wound on his neck disappeared. His eyes transitioned from black back to their normal color. Finally, he stood on all fours facing both of them as if they were strangers, growling and barring his fangs. Robert knelt in front of him and darted his eyes deep into his. Beauty stood motionless, unsure of what to think or do next.

"Hey, Buddy," he whispered restraining a smile, "From this moment on, you will do whatever Beauty and I say. OK... Now go on inside." When he stalked off into the house, it made Beauty more aware of what Robert had just done.

"You compelled him," she blurted. It was a stunning realization. After all, she had seen this thing done in the movies and read about it in those vampire novels but none of it compared to seeing the real thing done in person.

"You're still processing all of this, aren't you, my lady?"

"I am."

"Why don't we go inside – yeah. We've got a lot to get packed."

"Am I being compelled right now?" she asked playfully.

"Of course not. There's no need for that, now is there?"

The way her eyes shot straight into his when he said that told her how powerful he was. Then, he took her hand and they walked inside.

CHAPTER 7 – New Beginning

The next day the sound of the trunk of her SUV closing echoed through the woods just moments before they drove slowly over the dirt and rock pathway then pulled out onto the road.

"You look ravishing," he said smiling at her adjusting the radio station. The appreciation in his gaze always had a way of making her melt away.

"So, where are we going?"

"It's a surprise."

"I've sure been getting a lot of those lately."

"Have any disappointed you?"

She paused a moment with an innocent smile on her face then shook her head. "No, I can't say any have."

Her dark eyes met his and he admired them for a moment. Beauty did a little admiring of her own. There was something about the way his golden-brown eyes gazed at her that had a way of unwinding her. It was as if he could stare right into her soul and read her every emotion. She reclined in her seat and stretched out a little. The look in his eyes told her how crazy about her he was.

"You know love, I keep thinking that one day all of this – moving from town to town business will come to an end. However, the reality is that it will never be over. I need you to understand that," he said with seriousness in his voice. He glanced at her a moment before returning his eyes to the road.

Her eyes wandered out the window scanning the tall trees as they drove pass them. One of the things she admired about this region was how green it was; she knew she would miss it.

There was silence for several moments as they drove along the highway.

"I understand," she said softly, looking into his eyes.

He smiled at her with that halfhearted smile of his. *Her bravery is refreshing,* he thought. He knew she simply couldn't grasp the gravity of how complex the life of a vampire was. He didn't want this life for her. The thought of pulling over and letting her out crossed his mind but doing that would be like handing her over to death himself. *I changed her, now it is my responsibility to protect her,* he thought to himself. He deeply regretted the fact that he had needed to put her in so much danger to save her life. But he knew that, with time, he could teach her to protect herself. And he had eternity to do it.

They drove for five hours straight before pulling over into a gas station. Robert let Buddy run around for a moment at the side of the building, and then pumped the gas.

Beauty walked ahead into the store. The sound of the bell ringing when she entered made her more aware of where she was; it also alarmed the clerk that someone was there. She wandered down the aisle grabbing cold sandwiches and a couple bags of potato chips for the road. Then she heard the bell again when Robert entered. He walked straight to the front of the store, checked out the bathroom key, and then went around to it out back.

When she reached the end of the aisle, she glanced up into the mirror only to see her ghost-like appearance there. That was one of the downsides to being a vampire. People could still see her perfectly, but her own reflection of herself was barely there. She grabbed a few more items, some treats for Buddy, then walked to the front where she placed them on the counter.

"Hello; will that be all miss?" the young man asked enthusiastically as he sliced through a fresh apple.

He can't be more than twenty years old with that fair unblemished face and those light blue eyes, she thought. "Give me one second and I'll be right with you."

"Ah – shit!" he shouted in frustration as the knife slipped, cutting his finger. He immediately stuck his finger into his mouth and began sucking the blood from the cut; no doubt hoping to stop the bleeding.

"That's a nasty cut," she whispered, as his open wound suddenly became the focus of her attention. The smell of his blood did something to her. Her burning dark eyes filled with hunger, her veins pulsated beneath her skin throbbing with desperation. She watched him trying to stop the bleeding by wrapping a cloth around it. But, the more the blood seeped through the cloth, the more lost in the craving she became. Then the young man's eyes met hers.

"Are you okay miss? Why are you looking at me like that?" he asked with trepidation in his voice.

"Because your blood smells like the sweetest thing I've ever smelled and I want to suck every drop out of your body," she said as she looked him over.

"I'm sorry lady, I'm not into that kind of thing," he whispered backing away.

She could see the terror in his eyes, which only enhanced her thirst. Then, with a swift movement, she ascended to the countertop.

"Going somewhere?" She asked in a strong and slightly threatening voice.

She could hear his heart skipping beats. He reached for the knife but she knocked it clear just before her fangs pierced his neck.

When Robert returned, seeing what she was doing, he sped over the counter and pulled her away. He could smell the sweet essence of blood lingering in the air, not to mention seeing small pools of it on the floor.

The dark part of him wanted to join her but he had learned to control his cravings over the years. He leaned down and, staring into the young man's eyes, picked up a nearby towel and wrapped it around his neck.

"Keep the pressure on your neck, you'll be fine. You will not remember anything. Say it."

"I won't remember anything." The boy repeated, obviously dazed.

"What happened, Immortal Beloved?" He asked Beauty.

"All I remember is standing here checking out groceries and then he cut himself with the knife. The smell of his blood did something to me. I tried to fight it, Robert, I swear. But, I couldn't," she added.

"Shh - Shh Shh. Calm down now, it will be okay," he whispered as his eyes wandered the convenience store. "We have to get out of here," he said as he extended his hand towards her.

But she didn't take it right away. She flashed a wicked smile then pushed the groceries she'd left on the counter into a plastic bag. When her delicate hand took his, she squeezed it gently.

"Now we can go."

A few minutes later the sound of her SUV cutting through the wind whistled as they drove back onto the highway.

"So, how did you do it?"

"Do what?"

"Control the cravings? I saw you back there. Part of you looked like you wanted to join in but you didn't."

"Practice – my love."

She giggled, then sighed a deep sigh.

"I'm sure I'll need a lot of that because as soon as his blood hit the air, something came over me. Something I couldn't control."

"Listen – love. I don't want to mislead you in anyway – I'd be lying to you if I told you that I didn't feed." He hesitated a few moments, keeping his eyes on the road. "But you must learn how to feed."

"What do you mean?"

"I mean that young boy back there – he is not the kind I feed on."

"I don't understand."

He nodded and cracked a smile thinking of a better way to explain.

"The young man back there – he was innocent. I mean, he has evil in him – yes. We all do, but evil does not rule him. Those who are ruled by evil are the kind you should feed on," he said slowly.

Her facial expression told him she understood. "Well then. How can you tell who is who?"

"By listening with your senses, my love, that is what you should practice."

She smiled at him and held his hand while he drove for three more hours with Buddy in the backseat crying in frustration because he needed to feed. *Buddy will be so much easier than Beauty to train,* Robert thought to himself with a smile, *I can simply compel him to understand.*

She noticed a sign that read "Welcome to Lompoc" just before he pulled into the southern California town which was about 45 minutes from Santa Barbara. He drove down a couple of main roads, then took a couple of detours around a few run down back streets, then drove into an upscale, rich neighborhood.

"Wow, not a bad area at all," she said as they pulled in the luxurious, circle driveway.

"We're here," he said with a whisper and a hint of a smile.

"And where are we?"

"This is uh, one of my homes. I don't get to come here much but yeah – it's mine. I have an old friend who watches it while I'm away. She's uhh – she's one of us."

"She?" Beauty asked uncomfortably as a draft of jealousy slipped off her tongue.

"Relax, she's really cool; come on." His smile and reassuring voice was all she needed to follow him into the house. When they got in, he closed the door and noticed that the lights were off but the house was full of lighted candles.

He could sense someone was near. All of a sudden, a dark shadow shot across the room and up the stairs.

"Stay here, my love," he whispered before tiptoeing up the stairs in pursuit.

"Who's there? Come out, come out, wherever you are," he called out as the wooden steps squeaked with every few steps he took. "I'm older than you; I can feel it. I can smell you. Reveal yourself this second and if you don't – I – will – kill you," he exclaimed sharply.

Hardly a moment later the candles went out and the houselights came on.

"Well you spoiled all of my fun," a voice said firmly. And there she was, standing on the balcony looking down at them. "So serious all the time," she complained, and then continued, "Well, well, well. Look what the cat brought in."

A wave of relief came over him when he realized it was Jessica, his long time friend.

"Still making threats, huh?"

"I thought that might get your attention," he said sarcastically as he walked back down the stairs. "Come on down, Jessica. I have someone I'd like you to meet."

She ascended over the balcony then made a slow, magical descent to the floor with her fingers intertwined behind her. The twinkle in her eyes and the devious smile on her face told him she was sizing Beauty up. She could tell that Beauty was taken by Robert and was still in shock from her recent conversion.

"Jessica, this is Beauty; Beauty, this is Jessica my old friend from a hundred years ago. Don't worry; just friends," he repeated.

Beauty's eyes met his then met Jessica's in a long, deep catty stare. *Just friends,* Beauty thought to herself. *Who is Jessica really?* She wondered. *And what is she doing here?*

Beauty could tell her presence made Jessica uncomfortable from the way she tilted her head mischievously and her eyes widened with insecurity. She had a look on her face that said, *What is Robert doing with this pretty dark-haired woman?*

Jessica's burgundy hair flirted over her creamy, pale, skin. Her hazel eyes even flared with a hint of burgundy whenever she was curious, fascinated, or uneasy about something. And it was those burgundy tinged eyes that stared at Beauty with intrigue.

"Jessica!" Robert exclaimed, awakening her from a trance.

"Yes?"

"It's not polite to stare. I'm going to take Beauty to my room then you and I should have a chat out back."

A few minutes later, he closed the door behind him as they walked outside. It was just Robert and Jessica walking in the spacious back yard, which transitioned into a forest a hundred yards or so from the house. It was a beautiful night. The moon illuminated the dark night, reflecting its light through the slight fog that lingered between the trees.

"First of all, how did you get out of prison and what provoked you to come back here? With a woman; a very beautiful woman?" she added.

"Well, first I exploited a flaw in the prison system then I turned it around and used it to save someone's life. I believe humans call that magic." Robert explained. His pride was obvious in his voice.

"And her?" Jessica asked.

"Her, yes, she uhmm…" He paused a moment replaying the memory of what had happened in his mind. "She was dying Jessica. Cancer was killing her right before my eyes. What was I supposed to do?"

"You turned her?"

"Yes, I turned her. I turned her," he repeated with frustration.

"But that's impossible I still smelled the human scent on her."

"Well that's because I only turned her two days ago, Jessica; give it some time." He explained.

"You have feelings for her. I can see it all over her face," she accused, "And what now? I mean, she's going to have to feed," she whispered.

"I know this – relax. You're beginning to irritate me."

"Fine. What do you want me to do, Robert?"

"Now that's more like it," he said firmly in his strong accent, "just watch over her."

"Fine," she said blandly.

"I mean it, Jessica; watch over and protect her. She must never know about me and you – our past that is."

Twenty minutes later, he made his way back inside and into the bedroom where Beauty lay sleeping. He tried to be as quiet as he could but the faint sound of the door closing made her jump just a little.

"Those vampires sense kicking in already are they?" he asked, laying down beside her.

Her opening eyes met his warm smile as she shifted, resting her head on his chest.

"Tell me something, Robert."

"Anything for you, love."

"How did you manage to wiggle yourself out of prison to save me?"

Her question took him by surprise; it wasn't what he expected.

"Well," he said taking a deep breath.

She could see him thinking and replaying the images in his mind.

"Once upon a time there was a monster who loved to feed on innocent people. He liked doing unthinkable things to women and young men that were – unforgivable," he said. "He liked to violate youngsters that came to prison for the first time, taking advantage of their vulnerability," he added. "The strangest thing about the monster is the authorities kept releasing him, time after time and again, until, finally that monster met a fox. A cunning little bastard; too smart for their own good, those things."

She giggled a moment at the cleverness of his storytelling.

"And so, the fox waited for the perfect opportunity to present itself. An opportunity which when presented, the monster would only continue to do what it was compelled by evil to do. So, the fox set a trap for the monster and the monster took the bait. Now the monster cannot hurt anyone – ever again. The end," he said with a smile.

"You're crazy, Robert," she teased.

His warm smile met hers with a twinkle in his eye.

"Crazy like a fox" he whispered before planting a gentle kiss against her cheek then shutting off the lamp on the nightstand. "Good night –

Immortal beloved."

"Sleep well, my love…"

CHAPTER 8 – A Small Disagreement

The next morning, she got out of the bed and wandered down into the kitchen still half-asleep. The clock on the counter read 5:41 a.m. She ran her fingers through her hair, and then opened the refrigerator. Her eyes went past a large carton of milk and a bottle of orange juice to the bottle of apple juice hidden in the back. She pulled it free and closed the door. The sound of it shutting startled her a little but what sent chills up her spine was Jessica's devious face, just inches away, staring back at her. She had been standing behind the open refrigerator door. Jessica's burgundy eyes glittered with evil; she frowned at her and Beauty frowned back.

"Do you always wake up so early and wander through the halls, Beauty?"

She hesitated a moment, thought about what she said then shrugged her shoulders.

"Only when I catch an early morning thirst," she said, taking a sip.

"Ahh – yes. Don't I know all about those," she whispered. "Early morning thirsts," she repeated staring at Beauty's slim, perfectly sculpted neck.

This time Beauty could hear the wickedness in Jessica's voice as she said, "I get those from time to time but I usually quench them by drinking the life-blood from others."

"Listen, Jessica, I don't know what you think I've done to you that makes you so insecure but if you've got something to say to me – say it! Otherwise, stay the fuck out of my way."

Jessica cocked her head curiously, and then her eyes wandered devilishly up the length of Beauty's neck again.

"Careful, Beauty, it wouldn't require much effort to snap your neck in half," Jessica warned.

Then, in the blink of an eye, Beauty's swift hand came slapping her across the face.

Jessica touched the stinging sensation then quickly grabbed Beauty by the hair and threw her across the room. She crashed into the stove then hit the floor – hard.

The impact made her dizzy; Beauty could feel the room spinning in her head. Before she knew it, she could see Jessica standing over her and looking down at her with those evil eyes.

Then Beauty grabbed Jessica's leg and pulled on it hard. So hard that she fell backwards and hit her head on the floor.

"Would someone please tell me what the hell is going on!?" Robert shouted.

Beauty and Jessica were lying on the floor, both trying to regain their composure.

Suddenly Jessica stood up, her blackened eyes darting into his with anger. Then, before he could react, she jumped across the room and out of the window.

Their only clue as to where she had gone was the sound of shattering glass and the wings of pigeons flapping as her sudden exit scared them away.

Then his attention returned to Beauty. He quickly ran over to her. He could see her breathing heavily as she lay motionless on her backside.

"I'm so sorry, are you okay my love?"

"Where did she get her strength, Robert? That girl threw me across the room like a rag doll," she blurted, grunting as he helped her to her feet.

"Yes, Jessica can be a bit feisty when she doesn't get her way. It runs in the family."

"And what way is that?"

"I'm sorry, say again love"?

"I said what way is that? I mean, she acts as if you two were romantically involved or like I'm trying to steal you away from her."

He paused for a moment and his silence was not received well.

"Tell me that's not true, Robert?"

His eyes met hers with regret in them. She shook her head and dropped it a little.

"I can't believe this," she said sadly, throwing her hands up in the air.

"It was a hundred and twenty years ago if that makes you feel better."

"Why didn't you just tell me that when you brought me here?"

"Because I was trying to keep us from having this conversation and because I cherish the connection that you and I share – love..."

"She still loves you; you know that, right? I mean, at least give me that," she added when his eyes rolled across her face she could tell he was uncomfortable with the whole conversation.

"I think Jessica is uhh – what's the word I'm looking for, territorial at times but I wouldn't necessarily call that love. It's just in the vampire world, she's not used to me bringing other women around, especially a woman that I've turned. And something tells me, she thinks saving your life was a mistake."

"Did she say that?"

"No, I could just sense it a bit."

"Wow," she said taking a deep breath then taking a few steps away from him.

He quickly came up from behind her, wrapping his arms around her waist before kissing her twice gently on the back of her neck. "I hope you can find it in your heart to forgive me – my love."

She hesitated a moment, her eyes looking him over more carefully wondering if there was more to his relationship with Jessica that she didn't know.

"I forgive you, Robert," she whispered with a hint of reluctance and a vague smile. Still, it was genuine; she knew it and so did he.

CHAPTER 9 – A Pleasant Walk Spoiled

Later that night she slipped out of the house unnoticed and walked down the street. Then down another street, thinking of how much she missed Texas and how life was different here. Even the air smelled different she thought as she took a deep breath catching a bit of the pollen in it. And on this night, that was all she wanted - to get some fresh air and collect her thoughts after all the commotion earlier.

As she walked, she noticed the sound of music playing in the distance. It was coming from somewhere up ahead and she was quickly closing the distance to it.

"Johnny's Bar and Grill" the sign outside read and she entered with a solemn look on her face. The sound of Rock N Roll grew louder, and then quieted a little when her ears adjusted to being inside. She surveyed the patrons and noticed that it was a racially well-balanced place. The music reflected that diversity.

After a few moments had passed the sound of R. Kelly's *Your Body's Calling* came smoothly out of the jukebox – someone had dropped a few quarters in.

It was a youthful bar, she could tell not a single person there was over thirty-five and she was good about guessing someone's age.

When she reached the bar, she sat there a moment checking out a deer's head that was mounted on the wall.

"Can I offer you something to drink" a clean-cut, dark-haired man asked over the layered conversations around them.

"A Cosmopolitan would be nice." She replied.

"Sure, cumin right up."

When the bartender returned with her drink, she drank it and then ordered another. It was the first time she had drank alcohol since her husband died.

She sat there for an hour amused at how taken the men were by her beauty. She giggled to herself then out-loud and it was that last giggle that made her realize how tipsy she was. She caught herself rubbing circles around the rim of her glass and could feel the warm glow from the alcohol in her bloodstream.

"Mind if I sit down?" a voice said.

When she turned she met the eyes of a cute, dark-skinned black guy, with long braids in his hair done up in corn rows. She didn't encourage a lengthy stare. She turned away quickly after their eyes met and took another sip of her drink.

"It's a free country, I don't see why not," she replied.

"Thank you. You're not from around here, are you?" He asked.

"What makes you say that?"

"Because I've been coming to this bar everyday for the last three years and I've never seen you or, a woman as beautiful as you – ever. My name is Devante. Devante Brown."

"Nice to meet you, Devante," she said blandly and obviously disinterested.

"So do you have a name, beautiful?"

"Yes."

"Well?"

"That's it."

"What's it?"

"Beauty," she said sharply.

"Come on, you've gotta be kidding?"

"You don't believe me?"

"Not that; that's your name? Jason lemme get a beer … the usual and uhh … another Cosmo for uhh … Beauty."

"Listen," she interceded, "if you have any expectations for buying me that drink then you really shouldn't buy it. I do happily belong to someone," she added.

"Oh no, no expectations at all; just getting to know you a little. Some harmless conversation; nothing wrong with that, right?"

When their drinks came, she turned away for a moment to check the clock on the wall and, in that moment, he poured a white powdery substance into her drink stirring it quickly with a red straw.

"How about a toast, Beauty"

"Toast to what?" she asked raising her glass.

"To a fun-filled stay for you in this town."

Their glasses clinked loudly then Devante took a long sip from his beer and sat it down. Beauty put her glass to her lips and hesitated a moment keeping it there. She sniffed it, taking in the awkwardness of its distinct smell. Her expression told him he was busted. Then, she turned toward him and her drink went splashing across his face.

"Jerk!" She blurted angrily. "You better leave now before I scream and tell everyone what you just did." Her voice made it clear she was serious. Her eyes turned completely black and Devante was both startled and curious about it but too fearful of being exposed to linger.

He stood quickly, dropped twenty dollars on the counter and exited the bar. She sat there for another half-hour then her seductive frame strolled out the door. Her eyes wandered upward and were met by a sky full of stars. She thought about how beautiful they were and how tipsy she was as she walked slowly down the street noticing to how beautiful the neighborhood it was. She glanced down each alleyway of every block as she passed by.

Down one alley, she saw an elderly man sweeping as the fog lingered in the air around him. It had to have been at least midnight, she remembered thinking.

Just as she reached the next alleyway, she saw something that caught her eye through the thin veil of the fog that drifted in the air. She strained her eyes to focus on the image that was before her as the bright moon barely lit the recesses of the alleyway. It looked like a man had a woman pinned against the wall, ripping at her clothes.

"No!" the woman screamed desperately as Beauty began walking toward them. Then she saw the man's hand slap the woman hard across the face as his other hand wandered up the back of her skirt.

"Hey – stop that!" Beauty yelled, standing just a few feet away.

"Get lost lady or you'll be next." The man growled.

There was a brief silence as Beauty looked the man over more carefully realizing that it was Devante, the man she'd met at the bar.

"I said – stop Devante!"

The calling of his name got his undivided attention. Releasing the girl from his grip, he pushed her to the ground.

"You again," he blurted when his eyes met Beauty's.

Only this time her darkened eyes were full of hunger, and revulsion. Suddenly, she flashed through the air in the blink of an eye and sank her fangs deep into his neck. The sound of his screaming only made her hold him, frozen in her grip, longer. Finally she let him go and his limp body fell to the ground.

The taste of blood was intoxicating; the glow in her dark eyes said so as she wiped the blood from her mouth and her dark hair fell across her face. She drew it away from her eyes and then turned her attention to the frightened girl who was lying on the ground crying quietly. She could see the thirst and euphoria in Beauty's eyes as she came closer. Squatting down she stroked the girl's face gently.

"Please don't kill me," she pleaded.

Beauty was so far under the blood-spell that all she could do was think about how sweet and wonderful the girl's blood would taste.

"Don't be frightened child," she said slowly. "You can't be more than twenty years old; your skin is so youthful and soft. How old are you?"

"Nineteen," she whispered with reluctance. After seeing what Beauty had done to Devante, she knew she was about to suffer the same fate and she was terrified.

"What's your name?"

"Miranda."

"I'm so sorry – I don't want to kill you, Miranda. But this feeling, the power that blood gives me, is beyond my control."

"Please don't," Miranda cried, trembling violently.

"As much as I want to let you go Miranda, even more I want to drink every drop of blood in your body." She giggled a moment then rolled her eyes. "But you wouldn't understand that would you? You're human," she said as her fangs emerged. "I can feel your heart pounding in your chest. Forgive me Miranda," she whispered putting her fangs to the girl's neck and widening her mouth.

Miranda closed her eyes and braced herself. Then, out of nowhere,

Robert was there, wrapping his arms around her waist and snatching Beauty away. When the girl re-opened her eyes, she couldn't believe she was still alive.

"I think you've had enough fun for one night," Robert said keeping her against the wall. He could see the frustration in her face.

She was mad that he had stopped her from quenching her thirst.

"Alright now, calm down my love. Breath," he whispered sharply. He held her against the wall for a few more moments until her eyes returned to their normal color.

"Oh my god! Oh my god; I'm so sorry Robert. Did I hurt her?"

"No. It's lucky for you both that you have avoided disaster tonight." His eyes darted into Beauty's with a deep stare and the side of his fingertip brushed gently against her face.

She was turning even more – slowly evolving into something different.

He wondered how far out of control she would become and hoped he'd never have to bring himself to compel her into submission. That would be his last resort - taking her freedom away from her.

"Are you okay now?" he asked gently.

She nodded in agreement, as she gazed up into his golden-brown eyes, disgusted with herself at how violently she had behaved.

Then he blinked and gestured with his eyes toward Miranda. "The girl; she needs to forget what she saw. Would you do the honors, my lady?"

"Of course," she said, then walked over and stared into her soul, she spoke the words that needed to be *"spoken"* and Miranda, completely mesmerized, repeated them. It was the first time Beauty had ever compelled someone.

"Alright. Now run along, Miranda," Robert said, and her footsteps quickly faded into the distance.

CHAPTER 10 – Swimming in the Lake

The next day at noon, they strolled through the deep woods of his backyard, holding hands beneath the bright sun and blue sky.

She wore a beautiful yellow dress that blew in the breeze, baring the unblemished golden complexion of her shapely legs. She drew her dark hair from her face several times before the wind quieted.

Her beautiful dark eyes looked into his – her stunning eyes were one of the things that he loved most about her. They were the kind of eyes that spoke volumes; he could see the sweet innocence beneath the dark anger they hid. *She is 20% angel – 80% devil*, he thought. However, he knew most of that anger was caused by the death of her husband and having to ride the waves of hope and disappointment in the aftermath.

Robert could see something in her that was beyond beauty, something beyond those dark penetrating eyes that stared into the core of him. She was as beautiful on the inside as she was on the outside and it was his desire to bring more of that out of her. After all, her smile left him breathless, and no woman had ever made him feel that way before.

They had a mutual attraction for each other that stunned them both and the way they looked at each other would make anyone want for themselves what they shared.

"Is that a man-made lake?" she asked, breaking the silence.

"I made it myself, me and some old friends, many moons ago."

Then the most beautiful smile came over her face.

To see those dark eyes smiling and those pretty dimples made him as happy as he had ever been.

Then she pulled his belt free, dropped it on the ground, and began walking toward the lake. She had only taken a few steps when she stopped and looked back over her shoulder. Then she slid out of her dress and her bra, dropping them in the sand on the shore of the lake. Next, she bent over and slowly pulled her panties down, and then she turned around and threw them at him, giggling.

He watched her for a moment. Her pert breasts and beautiful brown nipples looked like ripened fruit ready for harvesting. Then she walked into the water as he lusted after her honey-gold cheeks before they disappeared into the water.

"Come on. Take your clothes off already; the waters not even cold."

A few moments later, he was there, together in the nude with her. Her sweet legs wrapped around his long frame as he held her close to his chest, cupping her soft bottom.

She kissed him with every part of her being while she surrendered in the arms of his protection. Suddenly she could feel his erection pressing against her. Then they became one as she slowly slid down onto him and they began making passionate love.

As the heated blood raced through their veins, their eyes went completely black with lust as both their movements and breathing grew more intense. They could hear the sound of the water splashing around their bucking hips and colliding bodies.

"I love you, Beauty," he said.

"I love you too," she whispered in the heat of the moment.

They made love passionately for thirty minutes before they both climaxed.

A beautiful black and yellow butterfly hovered over them for a moment before drifting off...

"You see, even the butterflies come for just a glimpse of your beauty my love." He smiled and she smiled back.

"How can you be certain it's not here for you, Robert?"

"Next to you? I hardly doubt it love," he said, fascinated with her, as they both stepped out of the water and put their clothes on.

"I still can't believe you got me to go skinny dipping." She smiled feigning her innocence.

"Well, there's a first time for everything. But you'd be surprised what I could get you to do." He said, completely missing the fact that she had just passed the blame to him.

"Oh – really?"

"Yeah. You little temptress." He said with a mischievous grin.

After he pulled up his long jeans and put his tank top on over his head, his eyes flashed at Beauty who was staring up into a tree at Jessica.

"Robert," she whispered, "She's been watching up there the entire time. What is her problem?"

"She likes to watch," he replied.

"Whatever, let's just go."

"Wait just a moment, Immortal Beloved. I have something for you." He put his wrist to his mouth and stuck his fangs into it drawing blood. It dripped into a small tube, which had a thin leather strap tied around it, that he held in his other hand. Then, he tied it around her neck.

"My blood; you will have a part of me with you always. Because I am one of the oldest vampires, it will save you if you ever find yourself in a desperate situation. It is far more potent than any other vampire's blood; all you would need to do is drink."

Her facial expression softened. "Thank you."

"Of course."

CHAPTER 11 – Treachery

As Robert turned to lead the way back up the path, the sound of a mild thud got their attention. Their eyes wandered down to the needle protruding from Robert's stomach, then up into the tree where Jessica was pointing some type of self-made bow and arrow at them. Her eyes were full of revulsion.

His eyes met Beauty's in a deep stare as he began breathing heavily. Then he pulled the needle free and his eyes closed completely as he crumbled to the ground.

Jessica climbed out of the tree, stuffing her hunting gear into a bag she had over her shoulder, and walked towards them. Robert's limp body was motionless as Jessica closed the distance with an evil smirk on her face that told Beauty this was not good.

"If you could see your stupid face right now," Jessica said, laughing at her. "So how do you feel now – Beauty? Perhaps the way I felt – yes? Alone? Betrayed? You can stop me anytime you'd like. Such audacity for you to come around here parading your good looks and then, having to watch the two of you make love. You disgust me," she added.

"Nobody forced you to watch you know. What do you want, Jessica?" she asked as her eyes scanned Robert's body for signs of life.

"Don't worry, he's not dead. Its poison," she said. "Just a little something to make sure he behaves himself since that seems to be impossible for him to do with you around."

"Jessica listen to me; you and Robert shared something once upon a time, I get that but, why can't you accept that he's moved on?"

"Shut up! Just shut up! I'm tired of hearing you speak!" Jessica yelled. "Make sure no one hurts her," she mocked, scoffing and then rolling her eyes. She ordered Beauty to help her carry Robert back to the house and together, they picked him up.

When they got to the cabin, they took him up to his bedroom and laid him across the bed with his hands at his sides as if he were lying in a coffin.

"Now, come with me Beauty; there is someplace I need to take you."

Beauty hesitated a moment, staring at him and debating what she should do.

"He'll be fine as long as you co-operate. I suggest you get moving."

Leaving Robert that night was hard for her to do. Seeing him lying helpless and unaware of his surroundings made her realize how much he needed her help.

Jessica drove her into town and stopped at a park where there was a college couple making out on a blanket they had spread on the ground. It was a dark night but the moon had come out to brighten the darkness just enough to make the young couple easy to see.

"Well, tonight we get to see how much you really love Robert. You see that couple over there kissing? I want you to kill them both."

"No, Jessica, you don't have to do this."

"I'm not doing anything Beauty, you are. Do it, or Robert dies. Which would you prefer?"

Beauty's head dropped into her hands, and then with a deep sigh, she said, "Fine." She got out of the car and disappeared into the shadows of the night.

Jessica kept her eyes on the couple lying on the blanket. Then the girl got up and walked over to the ladies' room. Seeing her opportunity Beauty entered the restroom a step behind her.

When Jessica closed her eyes and eavesdropped, she could hear the sound of Beauty's fangs penetrating the girl's neck; she never even got a chance to scream.

Beauty is a natural and she doesn't even know it, Jessica thought.

Then she saw Beauty's silhouette materialize from the darkness and walk over to the young man lying on the blanket. He rose to his feet as she approached with her head down, concerned that she appeared to be crying.

"Ma'am, are you OK. What's wrong?"

When she lifted her head, her eyes were completely black. The man's eyes widened and he froze; he could see blood around her mouth.

"I'm really sorry, but I have to kill you."

That was the last thing he heard before she drained him, and then broke his neck.

When she got back in the car, her dark, glossy, eyes met Jessica's as she closed the door. The exhilarating feeling that had come over her was unbelievable; it was a euphoric, blissful sensation caused by the new blood coursing through her veins.

"Well, look who's high on blood," Jessica taunted with a wicked laugh. "I wonder what Robert would think of you if he knew what you'd just done?"

Beauty was so intoxicated she couldn't respond right away. "I feel like my head is on fire, Jessica. Am I supposed to be able to hear what's going on down the street?"

"Beauty, Beauty, Beauty," she giggled, "welcome to my world." She watched her for a moment then began driving back home. She could tell Beauty was craving more.

"No! Wait! Stop the car Jessica; I want more!"

"Beauty, calm down," she said. "If I didn't know better, I'd think you were turning into an addict. What would Robert say if he saw you like this? Would he think you were a sweet girl or a blood-thirsty tart, huh?"

When they arrived back home, they went into the bedroom and saw Robert lying there motionless. They stood there a moment and just watched him; the way his long lashes hung over his closed eyes, he looked like he was sleeping. She turned to Jessica and said, "Alright, I did what you asked, now bring him back. Wake him up!" she demanded.

"Very well, a deal is a deal." Then she poured a clear liquid substance into his mouth.

"Come on Robert, wake up," Beauty whispered, wringing her hands.

Then he blinked his eyes open as he took a deep breath, gasping for air.

Beauty grabbed a glass of water next to the nightstand and gave it to him. "Drink this, babe."

When his eyes met hers, there was with a blank look on his face.

"Thank you," he said genuinely. "And who are you?"

Beauty's warm smile came swiftly, but Robert's expression didn't change.

"Jessica love, would you be a doll and grab my slippers? The leather ones," he added.

"I know which ones; the ones I bought you." Jessica replied.

Beauty realized that something was wrong. She followed Jessica into the other room and grabbed her by the arm. "Wait a minute. What did you do to him, Jessica? What's wrong with him?"

"Get your hands off of me! I'm just returning the favor – doing to you, what you did to me. Doesn't feel so good, does it?" Jessica replied.

Beauty sighed and rolled her eyes as Jessica took Robert's slippers out of the closet. Then she looked into Beauty's eyes and smiled.

"Well as you can see, looks don't always win – Beauty. So, now that I've won, now that I've beat you, why don't you do us both a favor and leave?"

When she returned to Robert a few moments later, he was standing shirtless and barefoot waiting for her.

"Ah, good girl. Thank you." He said, "I was beginning to wonder if you'd come back."

As Beauty walked into the room he stared at her a moment and then returned his gaze to Jessica. The way he looked at her cut Beauty to the core. The light and desire he'd once had in his eyes for her was gone.

"So Jessica, aren't you going to introduce me to your friend?"

"Oh, yeah; Robert this is Beauty. Beauty this is my boyfriend, Robert," she taunted slowly. "Beauty was just leaving..."

"No," he interrupted, "we have this big beautiful palace of a home. She should stay awhile, that is if she wants to and you don't mind, of course."

"No, not at all," Jessica said reluctantly.

"Actually I think I'd really like that Robert – thank you," Beauty said, smiling seductively.

Jessica flashed a dirty look at her, and then quickly recovered, careful not to let Robert see before he walked out of the room.

"Slut!" She spat with venom.

"Yeah? Well look who's talking." Beauty replied. "You didn't think I was just gonna walk away and give up that easily, did you?" Beauty said, making it obvious that she intended to fight for what she wanted.

Jessica didn't respond but her worried expression did. It was the first time Beauty saw fear in her eyes. The thought of making Jessica uncomfortable made her very comfortable.

This might not be so bad after all, she thought. She knew that this man was not the same Robert she had known before. This was all Jessica's doing and the sooner she found out what was wrong with him, the sooner she could try to heal him.

"Jessica love, why don't you bring your friend downstairs?"

Beauty could hear the curiosity in his voice and so could Jessica, that's what she was clinging to for hope. She had won his heart once and she had no doubt that she could do it again.

Downstairs, he had just taken a sip of champagne. Then he poured two glasses and handed one to each of them. Jessica stood next to him and pecked him on his lips and then she glared at Beauty with that "how-did-you-like-that" look.

Jessica kissing Robert didn't bother her as much as the fact that he kissed her back so easily and without a second thought. She had to remind herself that he was under the coercion of Jessica's spell and the kiss wasn't actually real. Still, it hurt to see it and it made her heart pound with jealousy.

"So Beauty," he said sipping his champagne and pausing a moment. "Tell me a little about yourself, why don't you?" When he said that, she could see a lustful flicker of light in his eyes. She knew that look; it was the look he gave when he was genuinely interested in someone. It was the same look he had given her when they first met.

"Well, I am Egyptian and African American. I grew up in Egypt most of my life with my parents Then my father brought us to America for a better life." She hesitated a moment as emotion filled her eyes. "Then I migrated to Texas where I later married a man who built a beautiful lake house where we lived happily until his untimely death. It was ten years ago that he died as I held him in my arms. I have lived alone in the lake house ever since."

There was a long silence after those heart-rending words.

"I am so sorry to hear that, Beauty; that is very unfortunate." Robert said with true feeling.

Hearing his words in his strong accent penetrated into the core of her. He had a way with words and knew how to project them with dramatic effect. She could see the compassion in his gold-tinged eyes as he stared at her.

Then he stood up and took another sip from his champagne glass as he gazed out the window into the night.

"That is a very sad and humbling story. May I ask how he died?"

She hesitated a few seconds, and then smiled gently, trying to keep herself from breaking down, "Cancer," she whispered, blinking back her tears.

When she said that, he closed his eyes a moment. She could tell that the word shot a pain throughout him. Her hope was that by some chance it would bring him back to the day that he saved her from that very disease.

"Maybe I'll use your story in one of my novels, with your permission of course. More life-changing stories such as yours need to be told," he added.

"So, you're an author?" She asked.

"Yes," he said with a chuckle. "I'm guilty of that." Then he turned to face her as Jessica looked on. "I'm sure after such challenging circumstances there must be some part of you that is void – yes?"

Her half-hearted smile at both his humor and how dead on he was marked her face. "I guess you could say that – yes," she sighed.

"I thought you might agree, which is why I'd like to offer you a place here; locked in the embrace of Jessica's and my love," he added.

There was a long silence at the end of his statement. She knew what he was implying and his comment scared her and turned her on at the same time. *This could be my way to get him back and destroy Jessica in the process*, she thought.

"Robert no," Jessica said. "I mean, I'm up for it, but not with her. Besides, I suspect she's a witch."

"I am not a witch!" Beauty exclaimed.

"Shh – Beauty," he murmured slowly putting his finger to his mouth. "Now – Jessica, that is a very serious claim that you're making, love. If you're right, we'll drink every drop of blood from her body. If you're wrong, you will either comply or she and I will drink yours, are we clear on that, darling?"

"Yes – Robert."

"Good."

"Now show Beauty upstairs, sweetheart – I'll be there in a moment."

A few minutes later, he walked into the bedroom to see Beauty and Jessica both sitting on the beautiful massive bed covered in burgundy and black satin sheets. There were five fluffy pillows scattered across it.

He took off his shirt at the foot of the bed and bit into his wrist with his sharp fangs. Jessica's eyes blackened completely at the sight of the blood running down his arm and so did Beauty's as they simultaneously lapped up the blood like kittens at a bowl of milk.

"Yes – Beauty, drink." he whispered as he slowly ran his fingers through her dark, soft, hair. Then his eyes darkened to black as the three of them were united in blood-lust.

When Jessica's eyes met his, she knew he recognized the betrayal which she attempted to disguise. She submitted by pressing her tongue against Beauty's neck and pulling on her nipples. Before she knew it, they were completely naked with Beauty's nipples in her mouth. Jessica's hands and tongue were all over her but Beauty didn't pleasure her back. She kept her attention on Robert kissing his chest, never breaking eye contact with him.

"That's right, Jessica; you've been a very naughty girl," he said, with his strong accent. "Worship Beauty's body and show her how sorry you are…"

Jessica's movements toward her became like a real worship session – sucking her breasts, neck and running her tongue along her private places from behind.

Finally, Beauty, with Jessica's help, pulled Robert onto the bed; it was like two lionesses attacking the alpha male. He was lying on his back when they started taking turns licking his erection. They stopped for a moment, spread his legs wider and got even more lost in the bliss, hissing and moaning with their fangs extended.

Then, he mounted Beauty from behind and had his way with her for several minutes while Jessica stroked his body. The height of their climaxes brewed, boiled and then, blissful releases came consecutively.

When she opened her eyes the next morning, Robert was lying beside her. She giggled when she looked at his handsome face not believing what she had done last night. His smile met hers with a hint of wickedness in it.

"Well, I guess you know now that I'm not a witch." She whispered.

"I knew all along that you weren't a witch." He said with a smile.

"But –"

"Jessica needed to be exposed, you needed to be loved and I –" he hesitated.

"What? You what?"

"I was the one that needed to do it." He said as they two into laughter.

She had a giddy look in her eyes as she gazed into the mystery of his.

"Do you remember when we made love at the lake house?"

"What did you say?"

"Oh nothing – forget it," she whispered sitting up.

"No, I heard you Beauty – but you said that as if we've been together before."

"You really don't remember do you? Robert we were together before. The day we met, we had a shoot out, I saved you then, you helped save Buddy. And then, you brought me back to life."

"Beauty stop it, stop it – Stop! You're being ridiculous."

"Very ridiculous," Jessica mocked sitting up from behind him, covering her breasts with the satin sheets. She had that stupid evil smirk on her face again.

Beauty dropped her head in her palms and shook her head in frustration.

"I can't believe this is happening." She whispered in frustration.

"Jessica, be a sweetheart and leave us for just a moment, would you"

"But Robert, I –"

"Jessica – please."

She rolled her eyes as she stalked off out of the room.

"Listen, I don't know what you're trying to accomplish by saying all of these things to me – but you have to pull yourself together, Beauty. Your scaring Jessica and you're scaring me…"

When he said that, she could see how serious he was by the disconnected look in his eyes.

"Okay – okay," she repeated in a whisper, "but I need you to tell me one thing, Robert."

"I'm listening."

"If a vampire was poisoned for some strange reason, how could the effects of that poison be reversed?"

He laughed for a moment then nodded in agreement. "Well, - if that happened, for starters you would have to…"

"Hey – hey," Jessica shouted as she rushed back into the room with a smile on her face.

Beauty glared at her and she glared back. Jessica could see the frustration on Beauty's face, knowing she had been close to learning how to bring him back.

CHAPTER 12 – Unknown Terrain

Later that same morning, the three of them saddled their horses and went for a ride out of the backyard and into the forest. The horses were moving eagerly over the dirt and rocks, showing how pleased they were to be out in the sunshine.

They had been riding for almost half an hour, admiring the beauty of nature around them as Buddy trailed close behind.

Jessica rode past Beauty looking back at her before weaving through the trees on her right.

Everything is a competition with her, Beauty thought.

They stopped their horses near a small creek running with ice-cold, crystal-clear, water. The sound of the water echoing as it ran over the rocks made Beauty smile.

Robert squatted down and washed his face in the creek before lapping up what he could as it ran through the palms of his hands. Beauty slid off her horse and did the same beside him.

"That's good water," he said looking over at her.

Jessica took a sip watching them closely out of the corner of her eye. Their chemistry made her uneasy; it was so effortless.

Sharing a drink, she thought, rolling her eyes over at them. It seemed that no matter what she did, they still found some way to be close to one another. She felt like they were on a group date and the thought of it made her cringe. When he touched Beauty's hand, her face filled with excitement. And there was that beautiful smile; the smile that had captured his soul not long ago.

When Buddy leaned over to lap up some water from the creek, Jessica patted him on his back, carefully examining how unnatural and exotic he was.

With a wicked gleam in her eyes she asked, "How did you manage to create such a beautiful creature, Beauty?"

There was a brief silence as their eyes met.

"Her husband bred him before he died," Robert blurted.

When he said that, she and Beauty's eyes met in a deep stare with the realization of what had just happened.

"When was that?" Jessica asked curiously.

"When was what?" he asked.

"What you just said about Buddy?"

"I don't know what you're talking about. You are becoming delusional Jessica. I didn't comment on Buddy, did I Beauty?"

She shook her head nonchalantly then looked at Jessica whose eyes flared with anger at her. The thought of Robert remembering something about her life, gave her hope. But for Jessica, it made her more determined to make sure it didn't continue.

"Let's stop with all the rubbish," he said in a whisper. "Beauty let me show you the cabin. Come on," he gestured with his hand as she, Jessica, and Buddy followed behind him.

They walked a short distance and, as they entered a small clearing, a large log cabin appeared through the foliage of the sparse underbrush.

"Wow, this is beautiful," Beauty said, stepping up onto the deck.

"Thank you," Robert said, "come inside and make yourself comfortable. Jessica, why don't you fire up the fireplace."

"Sure, babe." Jessica said with a sidelong glance at Beauty.

CHAPTER 13 – Time Travel

Several hours went by as they socialized, drank champagne and laughed in front of the fireplace. The three of them were pretty drunk by now. Robert staggered a little when he stood up and gestured for Beauty to follow him into the kitchen.

She walked in a few seconds behind him with her champagne glass in her hand as her dark eyes sparkled in the candlelight.

"You've created quite a life, Robert; you should be proud of yourself."

He sighed deeply and nodded in agreement blinking slowly. "Well, I'd be lying if I told you I wasn't a bit proud." His sweet accent made her giggle and smile that big beautiful smile he had always adored about her. Robert reached out and gently ran his fingers through her dark hair.

"You are a very special woman," he said pulling her closer until her body was against his. When he touched the side of her face, her breathing quickly grew heavier just before he planted a soft kiss against her lips. She closed her eyes for a few seconds and took in the dreamy moment. When she opened them he kissed her forehead, and then let her go.

"I want to show you something." He said.

Her beautiful smile emerged as he took her hand in his and ran his fingertips along the spines of the leather-bound books that were aligned neatly on the bookshelf on the wall. Selecting one, he stopped and pushed the top of it in.

The sound of a latch releasing could be heard as a trapdoor opened in the floor and, by the look on her face, he could tell she was intrigued. It was completely dark below as they stepped through the doorway. He continued to hold her hand, squeezing it gently as he led her down the staircase.

It's like walking down into an old basement, she thought. The sound of the stairs squeaking with each step and not being able to see heightened her listening ability. She focused as hard as she could to get a sense of anything that could give her a hint as to what they were walking into. She got nothing.

They took several more steps once they reached the floor. When Robert stopped abruptly, she bumped into him from behind.

"Are you okay, Beauty?"

"Yes, just a little nervous. Where are we? What is this place?" He hesitated a moment then kissed her cheek in the darkness.

"It's one of the places I like to come and meditate and explore possibilities," he added. "In our short time together, you've touched my life very deeply and for that I am so thankful." There was another silence but this time he could sense her smiling. "What if I told you it would be my honor to grant you two wishes? Anything you'd like," he added.

"You could do that?"

He sighed sharply then held both of her hands.

"It's not uhh – the traditional way of a vampire. Things are more modernized now, but as I said, I've been exploring. So yes, I have that ability."

"You said anything, right?"

"Yes," he whispered with a chuckle, "anything you'd like Beauty."

"My wish would be able to see my husband again."

He could hear the raw emotion in her voice combined with a longing for him. Robert closed his eyes and touched her face, wiping away the tears that spilled over her eyelids.

"And your second wish?"

She hesitated few seconds then, giggled. "For you to somehow give me the knowledge to restore your memory, even if you don't believe that you lost it."

He sighed briskly and playfully rolled his eyes.

"Don't be rolling your eyes at me." She said with a smile.

"How did you know that?"

"Because, I'm listening with all of my senses like you taught me, right?"

"You are a little sponge, aren't you? Okay Beauty, I shall grant both of your wishes. Are you ready to see your husband?"

"Oh yes." She said, almost afraid to believe.

"Then close your eyes now, love."

When she closed her eyes she saw a florescent color and there was silence for a moment, then he squeezed her hand gently and said, "You can open your eyes now."

When she opened her eyes, what she saw took her breath away. She was in a different time and place for he had transported them into a different dimension.

There was an endless field of beautiful green grass and endless fruit on every tree around. It was nighttime but the moon and stars lit this beautiful place.

There was no wind or sound just pure silence. Then, all of a sudden, the sound of an electrical charge broke the silence and there appeared before her the man she hadn't seen in more than ten years, her husband Robert. He was standing fifty yards away when she began running toward him for what seemed like forever. She jumped into his arms and wrapped her legs around him.

"Are you okay, Robert?" She cried.

"Oh, my God, I can't believe you're here." Her elated smile met his as he held her close for several moments. When he set her down she noticed his body was somewhat of a hologram, but she could still feel him; still touch him somehow. It was as if he was there but still had a faraway appearance. She thought she was hallucinating at first then, realized it was real – very real. Robert Moses watched them from a distance as they held hands with excitement in their eyes.

"Oh God, Robert I'm so sorry – if I could've done anything different."

"Don't be sorry, Beauty; you did everything you could." Tears ran down both of their faces.

Beauty looked around admiring the flawless fruit on the trees. "What is this place? The garden of Eden," she joked.

He smiled and admired the intrigue on her face.

"No sweetheart, it's Purgatory," Robert Moses said as he walked toward Beauty and her husband. When he got there, he stared at them together for a moment.

"Robert Moses, this is my husband Robert. Robert this is Robert. Wow that sounds strange," she said.

"Very nice to meet you, Robert; I've heard a lot of great things about you." Then, he turned away from them to give them some privacy. "Beauty, I hate to rush you but we only have a few minutes left before the gateway closes."

When her eyes met her husband again, he held her hands closely, "You like him, don't you?"

She nodded, slowly.

"I can tell by the way you look at him."

"I'm sorry honey – I just –"

"Shh – shh, don't be sorry. I've been gone from earth ten years and reality is I won't be back… But you, you're still young and beautiful. So much life ahead of you and you won't die for many, many years. I want you to be happy. He loves you back, yes?"

"Yes, he just doesn't know it right now. He's under a poison spell at the moment. It's a long story, but yes, he loves me back."

"Good."

Then, without warning, a roaring sound rang through the air as the florescent gateway transitioned to a blended mixture of pink and purple.

"Beauty," Robert Moses called out in an assertive tone. "It's time, love."

She turned to her husband and kissed him one last time. She closed her eyes and took in the moment her lips touched his. She knew it was the last time she would ever see him or be in his arms. He pulled away and looked to Robert, "Take care of her, please," he asked.

Robert Moses gently nodded in agreement. "Well, of course," he whispered.

Then, the ghost-like image of Beauty's husband flickered and disappeared. When she opened her eyes, they were back where they began, standing in the darkness in the basement of Robert's cabin.

Robert Moses ushered her back up the staircase.

Beauty closed her eyes as they were met by the blinding light in the kitchen.

When he closed the door behind them, the bookshelf closed.

Beauty took a deep breath and asked, "How long have we been gone?"

"About six hours." He replied.

"It felt like we were only gone ten minutes." She said in amazement.

"I know, that's uhh – one of the treats about defying time and space. The dimension for time changes," he added.

"I don't know how I can ever repay you for what you did, Robert - allowing me to see my husband and all."

"Don't be silly, Beauty; you don't owe me anything. I owe you. I know you didn't want to have the threesome with Jessica. I saw it in your eyes and yet you still agreed to it – why?"

She tried to restrain a gentle smile but it managed to overcome her sweet face. "Because you're not yourself right now and love is such a selfless thing; the most powerful magic in the world. It'll make you do stupid things, Robert."

Then his handsome smile met hers. "I'm sorry, darling, did you just say love?"

There was a brief silence.

Beauty walked over and stood in front of him, wrapping her arms around him. "Yes I did. I love you, Robert Moses."

He stared down into her beautiful dark eyes, putting his mouth to hers. He kissed into the core of her while the euphoric bliss passed between them. His aura was so powerful that she couldn't have pulled away even if she had wanted to. It was as if a magnetic force bound them together.

Suddenly, she felt a shift of energy come over her; her senses told her something was wrong. When she opened her eyes, she saw Jessica standing behind him injecting something from a needle into his neck.

Robert fell to the floor and started convulsing. He shook frantically for a moment and then became motionless.

"Jessica, what the –"

"I told you to leave, but you just wouldn't listen, would you?" Jessica screamed at her. "Now, you will have to experience what it's like to have your heart ripped right out of your chest. Buddy – come here," she said, clicking her tongue at him.

"No! What are you doing Jessica?" Beauty cried.

"Shut up already, Beauty! Just shut up! I'm ruining your life like you did mine. That's what I'm doing!"

Buddy walked into the kitchen and stopped in front of Jessica. Then she smacked Robert across the face until he opened his eyes a little. "Robert, darling, I need you to tell Buddy that he's solely under my control now and to do only as I tell him." Jessica said.

"Do what she says Buddy but don't hurt Beauty," he said staring deep into Buddy's eyes.

"No, Robert, no!" Cried Beauty.

"Say another word and I swear, I'll drive a stake through his heart right now! Now Buddy, I want you to go out and kill every human within twenty miles of us. When you are done, return to me. Now – go!" Jessica shouted.

Buddy wandered out the front door and into the woods.

Jessica looked at Beauty and giggled. "I love seeing that stupid look on your face. It pleases me so much," she added.

"Now what? Do you feel better about yourself? Feel like you've done a great service to the world killing so many humans? You know, it doesn't matter what you do, Jessica, Robert will never look at you the way he looks at me. Not even under the spell of that blood poisoning. Are you pleased about that?" Beauty taunted her.

Jessica's eyes quickly transitioned from a deviant smile to pure evil. She didn't appreciate being chastised by a newer, weaker vampire. She flashed through the air and kicked Beauty in the chest, sending her flying out the shattering kitchen window and onto the porch deck outside!

The powerful impact knocked the wind out of her. Beauty turned on her side and tried to catch her breath. The broken glass fell from her lap onto the wooden deck. As she started to crawl away, Jessica put her foot on her bottom and pushed her back down.

"Look at you; crawling like a whore, you bitch." Her wicked laugh echoed through the forest as Beauty got to her feet. "Still wanna run your silly little mouth? Maybe, I'll go back in there and just end Robert's life now," she added.

"No. Whatever you want, I will do it Jessica. Just promise me you won't hurt him." Beauty said.

Just as she said that, Beauty noticed twelve men mounted on horses watching the exchange between her and Jessica. These men must be vampire hunters she told herself.

One of the men slid off his horse and walked towards them. He stopped next to Beauty but then his eyes met Jessica's eyes.

"Take the girl. Do whatever you want with her, and then dump the body." She told him.

It was a stunning realization of what was about to happen.

"Wait, Jessica; please," she said as the man grabbed her arm. Her heart was pounding in her chest and her nerves were all over the place. "I know I've driven you to feel this way so I won't resist my fate. But please, please let me see him one last time. To say goodbye," she added.

There was a brief silence, she could see Jessica thinking, debating with herself if she would allow it or not. "Fine," she said sharply. "Give her a moment alone with him. But watch her," she said as the man escorted her inside and stopped at the kitchen entrance.

When she saw Robert's motionless body on the floor, she knelt down next to him and tears began spilling over her eyelids. "I'm so sorry, Robert; I failed you," she whispered as she ran her fingers over his handsome face. "I thought so hard but I couldn't figure out how to reverse the blood poisoning. Please forgive me, darling, I love you." Her dark eyes wandered across his face as she leaned over and slowly kissed his soft lips. Then it hit her from out of nowhere as her fingers fidgeted over the glass tube of blood around her neck. It was the necklace he given her at the lake. She replayed in her mind what he told her, *"If you ever find yourself in trouble, use this."*

The horseman snapped his fingers a few times. "Get on with it lady; we don't have all day." He said harshly.

Beauty unscrewed the tube from the clasp of leather and quickly poured the blood into Robert's mouth before she pulled away.

As she walked out the front door and passed Jessica, Beauty asked her what she would do with Robert?

"I don't know yet, Beauty. Kill him? Maybe strip him of his powers first," she laughed. "Take her away in that carriage and him to the rendezvous point in this one. But first, shackle his hands," she added. "Keep him restrained at all times and I don't want anyone talking to him. He's proven to be very convincing at times."

A few moments later, their loaded carriages maneuvered through the misty forest. The clomping sound of their horses' hooves over the gravel gave a sense of how powerful and important this unknown mission was. They had ridden for an hour when the carriage that held Beauty turned off of the road onto a pathway while the one Robert was in continued ahead.

Inside, Robert's limp body shook back and forth from the bumpy ride. Then his eyes blinked open and he looked around until his powerful scream cut through the forest like a man who had awakened from the dead.

The six-carriage entourage stopped abruptly as Jessica stepped out of one and looked back at the one Robert was in.

"What in the hell was that? Who was that screaming?" She asked.

Suddenly the carriage door swung open, banging violently against the side of the carriage.

Jessica could feel her henchmen's hearts pounding in their chests as they gathered next to her. They stared at the door hoping that Robert Moses would not step out - but he did. The first thing they saw was his dark, shiny, steel-toed boot as it touched the ground.

Jessica swallowed nervously and watched him stand and straighten his back. His eyes were already completely black when they met hers. She could see the hunger and anger in them and feel a strength in him that wasn't there back at the cabin.

By this time all twelve men had un-holstered their guns and pointed them at him. Robert stopped just in front of them.

"To the mortal men that stand before me, you should know that I am not mortal. It would insult me for you to fire your useless weapons at me," he said. "There is only one life that needs to be taken today and that is our dear friend Jessica, which is why I'm prepared to spare your miserable lives if you will drop your weapons and walk away now," he said. Becoming silent, he waited for their reply.

They looked at Jessica with a *what-do-we-do-next?* expression on their faces.

"Don't just stand there like idiots, shoot him!" she shouted and then wild bullets began flying through the air hitting him, only for his wounds to heal instantly.

Robert closed his eyes and disappeared.

The horsemen's eyes scanned the forest for him. Suddenly, the bite marks from his fangs appeared on one of the men's neck as he screamed. The others shot seven rounds at him, realizing they had put seven holes in their friend instead of Robert.

Robert then took another and another. The only evidence of his presence was his fangs crunching into their necks and the screams of dying men before their bodies hit the ground.

While Robert picked each one of them off violently, Buddy returned to Jessica. She nodded and ran her hand across his head gently petting him Although it appeared to be a gentle petting, what she was really doing was extracting and replaying the images from his mind of all the humans he had killed. "Good boy," she whispered wickedly as she pushed a wooden stake threw his heart. He collapsed and began whaling until his screams eventually faded to silence. He was dead.

Disgusted at what she had done, Robert flashed through the air and drove a stake through her stomach.

She stared deep into his eyes as she bled from her mouth. Anger and sadness filled him. After all, once upon a time, before Beauty, she was his woman. How did it come to this he wondered? In the depths of his heart, he knew it was the pure jealousy of Jessica's broken heart. He held her up against the carriage in disbelief.

"You missed my heart," she said, "Why? Just kill me and get it over with; do it!"

He pulled the stake from her stomach and threw it across the woods. "After what you've done, that would be too easy for you. You will live today, not remembering anything that happened here, and you will do everything I say. Do you understand? Now repeat it," he said staring into her soul. When she repeated his instructions, he let her go and pushed her away.

"Oh my god, Robert; my stomach; what happened?" She asked.

"Oh, just a couple of lads trying to have fun with you; you put up a good fight but I had to finish them off. I saved you, love," he said with a smile. "Now saddle up with me; they have Beauty. We must go."

CHAPTER 14 – Turbulence 2

Moments later, they sped through the forest in passionate pursuit to find Beauty. They rode fast for fifteen minutes until they made their way to the next village. There she was; shackled with her hands in front, as four men grabbed at her bottom and pulled at her clothes.

"Hey, stop that right now!" he shouted sharply pulling in closer to them as Jessica followed. His brown eyes looked around to measure the danger. With his gun (an old-school .38 handed down from his father) drawn, he walked his horse in circles around them in frustration.

There was silence; the only thing that could be heard was the horse's hooves clomping over the dirt.

Robert's eyes briefly met Beauty's gaze before he returned his attention to the four men. He knew he had to be careful. It was looks like that from Beauty that made him weak, and at a time like this, such a distraction could get him, or her, killed.

"Gentlemen, there are some things I'll needing from you," he said.

"Our food, our horses?" one of them asked.

"I don't want your food and I don't want your horses. But I will need that woman."

When he said that, they looked at Jessica with confusion. After all, it wasn't long ago that she had handed Beauty over to these same men to be ravaged and killed.

"What's in it for us?" One of the men asked.

There was a brief silence. Robert stopped his horse. Jessica cocked her gun and watched over Robert waiting for him to give the word. His eyes blackened for a moment before they returned to their normal color. He tried to disguise his impatience, but it was in his eyes. "Perhaps I'd be gracious enough to spare your life." He said flatly.

There was a long silence and the older man in charge turned to the other men. "Cut her loose," he said sharply.

When she was free, Beauty quickly climbed onto Robert's horse and wrapped her arms around him.

By the look on their faces, you could see the men were just as stunned as Beauty was. After all, they had every intention of enjoying her and then throwing her away. That is until Robert came along and took their lunch away.

"To keep you from getting any bright ideas, I will also need your horses, but not for me to keep," he added. "They'll be saddled and unharmed a mile ahead, you have my word."

Those were his last words before he whistled at Jessica and they rode into the forest with Beauty's arms around him. Several minutes later, they stopped and tied the horses then continued riding until their horses climbed to the top of a hill where they stopped. They slid off and sat on the hill that overlooked a small lake. Robert took his canteen from his horse and sat down between them and took a drink. He turned his attention to Beauty as the sun slowly began to disappear in the distance.

"You came for me," she gently whispered.

"Yes, I came for you, my lady." His smile and her smile were one.

"What did you just say?" she asked remembering the last time he said that was when he rescued her at the lake house.

"I said I came for you, my lady."

It was in that moment that Beauty understood his memory was fully intact. "You remember," she said putting her mouth to his and kissing him deeply. She pulled away and stared at him a moment with her eyes sparkling. The look in his eyes confirmed to her that he was back.

Before, he had looked at everything as if he didn't know what it was but now, she could tell he was there with her. While Robert and Beauty became re-acquainted, Jessica watched them but thought nothing of it. After all, she was under his compulsion.

"I have something I must tell you, Immortal Beloved."

"Thank you for saving me, Robert. Now let's go back and get Buddy and go home."

"I have something I have to tell you," he repeated. "It's Buddy; he's dead."

"What? What do you mean he's dead?"

"Listen to me, Jessica took Buddy … she killed him; I'm sorry. The reason she's being so nice is because I compelled her to help me find you so I could deliver her to you, my love."

Beauty's eyes darkened with anger before reverting to their natural color. "She – killed – my dog?"

"Yes, and now it is your turn to return the favor." He called out Jessica's name and when she came close, he stared in her eyes seductively as he cut her neck with his fingernail. "Don't move," he whispered as he handed a stake to Beauty.

As blood ran down Jessica's neck, Beauty's eyes went completely black and the veins beneath them pulsated under her skin.

"Jessica, your behavior has been absolutely unacceptable. To be quite honest with you, it has been rather disgusting," he said.

"Betrayal after betrayal," Beauty interceded taking a few steps before stopping in front of her. "And to think I wanted to get along with you."

The look on Jessica's face was marked by fear. The sight and smell of her blood alone was intoxicating to Beauty; her heart kicked up a notch in her chest and so did Jessica's - but not for the same reason.

Then, Robert's calm reassuring hand touched her on the shoulder. "Look at that fountain of blood running down the traitor's neck," he said. "Would you do the honors, Immortal Beloved? Go ahead, drink my love…"

And it was that fragment of encouragement she needed that sent her fangs piercing slowly and deeply into Jessica's neck. She held her still a moment, taking in the euphoric blood-lust sensation as Jessica's blood raced through her bloodstream.

Robert stood behind Beauty, kissing the back of her neck gently as if he were consoling her while she drunk every drop of Jessica's blood. It was so good, she couldn't stop - even when there was nothing left.

She broke Jessica's neck so thoroughly that she was completely decapitated. Beauty held Jessica's head in her hands as her body fell to the ground.

Beauty dropped the head, then turned and faced Robert. Her dark eyes were so beautiful as they sparkled from the euphoria brewing inside her.

Robert bit his wrist and placed it against her mouth. She sucked on it hard until he pushed her away.

She took a few steps back, spun around in a circle, and then ascended into the air. She stayed there, hovering thirty feet in the air as she looked down at him.

He smiled that beautiful smile of his, staring back at her in amazement. He knew it was his blood that gave her the power to ascend. Robert crouched down and leaped into the air where he met her. There, they held and kissed one another, suspended in time, in the lock of an embrace. When he pictured a beautiful day in the forest at the lake house, they were there – floating and walking on air like two angels in the sky.

They were so overtaken by passion that Beauty accidentally bumped her head and let him go. They both fell to the ground and burst into laughter flushed with pleasure. The rays from the sun shinned beautifully through the spaces between the leaves and branches.

Robert laughed and smiled as he watched the joy that it brought her to be at home again.

She walked up to him and kissed his lips.

"You transported us here in five seconds; can we stay, Robert?"

"I'm afraid not, love. I mean, don't get me wrong; I'd love to but we still have those vampire hunters to worry about. They'll be back here; trust me, they're tyrants."

"Alright, well at least let me go inside and grab a few things."

"Of course, my lady," he whispered taking her hand and walking with her up the porch steps as she fondled her keys.

"Oh damn; which one is it."

His eyes wandered suspiciously over the lake house, inside the window and the forest around them. "We've gotta hurry, sweetheart; something's not right," he said as she pushed the door open and stepped inside.

"You should've let me go first," he muttered walking behind her but was kept from entering. She turned around and noticed he wouldn't come inside.

"Come on already, what are you waiting for?" She asked.

"I can't come in," he said, sharply with frustration written on his face.

"Why not?"

"Because I'm here to keep him out," a man's deep voice said as he appeared from around the corner and stood behind Beauty.

"Oh my God; Robert, help me," she said. Her terrified scream pierced the air around them.

"Relax, my love." When Robert saw the six foot six inch man standing behind her he shook his head in disbelief; it was a familiar face.

"Bilial." he said, "And what brings you to the outskirts of Texas?" As he spoke, his mind went back to happier times when he and Bilial were kids and both learned what they were – himself a vampire and Bilial a witch, practicing their skills and magic together.

Bilial was a tall black, hulk of a muscle; no one had ever defeated him – not ever. He was 275 lbs of solid muscle that showed underneath his clothes. He was bald with very dark skin; he looked like a perfectly sculpted African warrior.

"It's you that has brought me here, Robert. If only I could count all the witches you've killed, you blood drinker. Now you can suffer as we have suffered," he spat, his strong, deep, voice reverberating through the woods as he wrapped his arms around Beauty's neck.

The terror in her eyes darkened Robert's with anger. "You speak of those witches as if they were saints, Bilial, but they performed witchcraft that killed vampires that had never killed humans or witches. I guess that's the part you like to leave out."

"Now you can suffer as we have suffered," Bilial repeated viciously.

Robert ran his tongue over his elongated fangs. Then, a strong wind blew his feet out from under him, blowing him backwards. He grabbed the ledge on the porch to keep from being blown away completely. All of his body except for the arms that held him there was suspended in the air as the vicious wind blew across him.

Bilial's grip tightened around Beauty's neck as he watched Robert and laughed.

Suddenly, Robert let go of the ledge. The wind blew him back about twenty feet but somehow, magically, he hovered for a moment then literally began walking on air back toward the porch. Within a split second, he was standing back at the door, the wind still blowing across him, only now, it had no effect.

The expression on Bilial's face quickly changed from confidence to worry. He turned and walked into the house.

Robert's movement quickened; he was at the back of the house in a flash; there are no creatures faster than vampires are. Gazing through the window, he saw the fear in Beauty's eyes as Bilial took her upstairs. Robert flew up to the second story, landing on the terrace and saw them as they entered the room. He punched the window hard sending glass everywhere; he was still unable to enter the house.

When her eyes met his, he did the only thing he could to break the invisible wall keeping him at bay, it was a desperate attempt but it was all he had left. He moved his lips knowing she would eavesdrop in on his words. "Tell me I have permission to come in," he whispered, "Tell me, love."

"You can come in, Robert; you have my permission." She whispered to him.

Without warning, the wind abruptly stopped and Robert was through the window in an instant. He pulled Beauty free and shoved her behind his back. He stabbed Bilial in the stomach, then in the heart and finally, stabbed him in the skull before piercing his neck with his elongated fangs. Blood splattered everywhere as he drank him dry twisting his head completely off his body and throwing it against the wall. With his eyes still blackened, Robert turned to Beauty, wiping the warm, dripping blood from his mouth. "This is what I will do to anyone who tries to hurt you. God forgives; I do not, my lady."

She drew closer to him. The pink tip of her tongue emerged and traced over his full lips, tasting the blood from his mouth. Her eyes joined his with darkness reeking of lust.

"You are everything that is good," he said, pressing her soft breasts into his hard chest.

"I love you, Robert," she whispered, backing him into the wall until her legs fit between his, cradling his growing erection. She massaged it from outside his pants; she could feel it throbbing. Then, in one motion, she pulled and ripped off his clothes.

He did the same to her.

Her eyelids dipped to half-mast as she stroked him in her hand for a moment admiring his features. Then, without warning, she leaned down and rode his erection with her mouth. She bobbed her head up and down slowly as he wrapped a fistful of her hair around his hand. His breathing grew heavier as she jerked his erection with long strokes in her mouth. He ran his hand up the back of her thighs, over her smooth bare ass and then gave her a firm smack across her cheeks.

Hearing Beauty moan with a mouthful of him overtook him with passion. He lifted her up in his arms carried her over to the bed and eased her down on his erection. He could feel her inner walls squeezing down on him as she rode him. He cupped her cheeks bottoming out on him every time she went down. Then he rolled her over, spread her legs as far as they would go and pounded into her as if it was his last day on earth.

Her nipples rubbed his chest as their bodies collided in unison. It was heaven, he thought, feeling their skin-on-skin as they made love.

She cooed underneath him while he hammered away inside her with a grip around her like an eagle on its prey.

"You're heaven, sweet," he whispered between shallow breaths.

They went at each other for half an hour until her climax erupted just before his and he poured himself inside of her, collapsing on top of her.

They laughed for a moment laying there foolish over one another and then got dressed.

"What now? What's next on the agenda?" she asked with a smile as she drew her beautiful dark hair behind her ear.

"We should probably get back to California as soon as possible. Staying here is suicide, love. They'll be back and I can't risk losing you."

"Why was Bilial so angry with you?"

He scoffed at the thought of the question. "Because Bilial believed it was okay for witches to kill innocent humans and vampires for fun and that witches shouldn't suffer any consequences because of that. I told you love; it gives me no pleasure draining the life from an innocent human. However, I will happily take it when they are ruled by evil. I told you that before, remember?"

"I remember. I admire your confidence and I admire your honor, Robert. You are a noble man," she added.

It was then the depths of his character resonated with her as he paced back and forth in front of the window. He was light and dark she thought and somehow baring witness to his dark nature just moments before gave her a true sense of protection. She knew he would slay any man that tried to take her away from him or that ever thought to harm a strand of hair on her head. Just as quickly as he would take a life, he would try to save one for the right reasons.

Their relationship had blossomed over the past few months. She thought about the day their eyes met in the misty forest and how fragile she was emotionally. The death of her husband had truly left her shattered and part of her always felt traitorous for letting Robert in; but the truth was that he had charmed her and stolen her heart.

"That's a big smile," he said awakening her from her trance. His caramel skin was so luminous that it glowed. His lashes were long, his eyes shined like gold and then there was his disgustingly handsome face. "Let us go now, love."

She followed him as he stepped out onto the terrace. He picked her up and leaped into the air. They soared nearly fifty feet into the air before descending slowly and hearing the sound of their feet touching the ground.

They stood motionless for a moment; her eyes peered up at him.

He touched her face then ran his fingertips over her bronze skin as he kissed her lightly on the lips. She giggled flashing her beautiful dark eyes into his as she drew her silken hair from her face.

Robert grabbed her hand, jerked her into motion and smiled. Robert and Beauty raced through the trees like two little kids with twigs slapping their faces.

It is like heaven being with her, he thought to himself. He wrapped his arms around her and whispered in her ear, "Close your eyes, my lady."

CHAPTER 15 – The Battle

When she opened her eyes a few seconds later, she realized he'd teleported them back to California.

"It's night time here; how did you do that?"

"Some secrets are better best kept," he murmured.

Her beautiful, soft, expression quickly filled with horror when she noticed six men dousing a fire in the surrounding forest.

"It's them!" one of the men yelled as their horses stampeded towards them.

Robert was just as shocked as she was, his eyes darted around suspiciously as one of them unloaded his shotgun at him. He leaped into the air, slit the man's neck open in midair with his claw, and ducked an arrow shot at him as soon as he hit the ground.

Beauty ran her tongue over her elongated fangs and her dark eyes blackened. She increased the speed of her steps, flashing through the air and sinking her teeth into a horseman's neck. Then another, she decapitated hovering in midair catching him from behind just before her feet hit the ground.

Robert glanced at her and, as he pulled the knife from a horseman's stomach, he admired the ferocity that she brought into battle. She sent the blood splattering from a man when she bit his neck open; the light from the fire illuminating the sweet blood.

It was that man, that both of them clung to a side of his neck and feasted on his body. They savored every sound he uttered, every move he made, tightening until the very last beat of his heart stopped. It was bloodlust.

Then, they both stood up, wiping the warm, dripping, blood from their mouths. They were intoxicated from the bloodlust brewing in their veins.

He stepped closer to her; their eyes still completely black, fangs still elongated. He pulled her jeans and panties down and away from her body. She stood, naked from the waist down, in the dark forest lit only by a fire that burned the area around them.

The sound of the fire crackling over the trees only added to their arousal. She cut through the air with inhuman speed and while standing behind him, took his clothes off and kissed the back of his neck.

Oh how beautiful it was to see how quickly, yet seductively, he flew through the air taking off her shirt and then her bra. One moment he had been in front of her licking her hard nipples, running his hands up the back of her thighs. The next, he was behind her. He could have sliced her throat if he wanted and she could have done nothing to stop him. But there was no anger in his glare, only passion and lust.

She faced him then pushed him to the ground and hopped on top of him, pinning his shoulders in the dirt with her knees. Her beautiful hair brushed his cheeks; fire blazed in his eyes as he licked his lips. Then, he rolled over and was on top of her. Her dark eyes gazed into his. She could feel his erection growing and pressing against her feminine core.

Then he groaned a sound that was not of pleasure; panting on top of her. Lust was no more; his eyes filled with pain as he stood up and turned around.

Within an instant, Beauty rose to her feet and put her clothes back on and then Robert's pants. When she focused, she saw a needle sticking into Robert's back and a man standing there with an arrow still in his hand. She realized that they must have missed one in the heat of feasting.

She pulled the needle free and threw it across the forest.

"That won't do him any good now," the horseman said. "He's got about one minute before he's helpless…"

She lunged towards the man but Robert quickly shoved her behind his back with the little strength he had left. It was then she realized that this horseman wasn't just a horseman; he was a vampire hunter.

Robert tried to fight off the effects of the paralyzing poison racing through his veins but his knees gave out and he collapsed. He panted for several moments; his eyes rolling into the back of his head and then he went silent – completely silent.

She hissed at the sight of seeing him that way. Her fangs elongated as she sized up the horseman. *Could I rip his throat out before he can shoot one of those needles into me?* she wondered. "How did you find us?"

"Well, in all fairness, he hid you well. But – uhh – Jessica put us on your trail not long after you got here. After she realized the two of you were an item," he added. "Well, quite honestly I want the reward money that's being offered to deliver him to the queen."

"What queen?" She asked. This was the first she had heard of any queen.

"The queen witch. Now don't go getting any ideas. If I don't give him another shot soon, he will die and not even you can bring him back. So get rid of those fangs and I will spare you. What do you say?" He asked seductively.

She would do anything for Robert. The thought of saving his life was a no-brainer. Her fangs quickly receded into her mouth and her eyes returned to their normal color.

The hunter shot a needle straight into her chest and she collapsed.

"You sure are a stupid bitch," he blurted walking over to them. He loaded them into his carriage, smacked his horses' bottoms and disappeared into the forest.

CHAPTER 16 – New Beginning

(The Queen Witch)

Twelve hours later, Robert's eyes opened. He blinked rapidly, trying to shut out the stinging light and see through the haziness at the same time.

The horseman peered down at him and then laughed.

"You're still alive. That's good; ain't no reward for a dead vampire." He joked. "I even brought your girlfriend along."

When he looked around, he saw Beauty lying motionless. If his heart could have, it would've tore in half at that moment. He hissed loudly but his fangs did not emerge.

"Yeah, I know – I know, if you could, you'd probably rip my heart right out of my chest right now, wouldn't you? But that ain't gonna happen because you're weak, boy; it's the blood poison I shot you up with. It drains your strength. What you need is blood, but you ain't gonna be getting any of that where you're going."

They rode awhile longer then pulled into an old palace deep in the woods off the side of the road and down a seldom-used pathway.

It is enormous, Robert thought as the carriage stopped in front of it. His eyes rolled over Beauty's dark silken hair; her skin was pale from the poison that held her unconscious. That was his last thought before the squeaking sound of the door swinging open drew his attention.

The man who'd brought them there stuck a needle in Beauty's arm and pushed. Within a few seconds, her eyes blinked open and she took a gasp of air.

"My love, my love," Robert whispered while cradling her body next to his.

"Alright, get them out," the horseman ordered the men rushing out of the palace. "Put her somewhere and take him to the queen."

When the guard grabbed her arm and pulled her outside, the reality of what was happening set in. They were being separated and it might be the last time they saw each other.

"No! Robert!" she screamed. Her scream echoed in his ears as he watched the hot tears pouring down her face.

"I love you, Immortal Beloved; you are everything that is right, my lady."

Then she was led away, their eyes never breaking contact until she finally disappeared inside the palace.

"That must be them; they're here," the queen told her crony looking down on them as they stood out on the terrace.

Robert was escorted out of the carriage and inside by the man who had captured him. He was shackled at his ankles and wrists and was so weak, he could barely walk.

Robert kept replaying the sound of Beauty's screams in his mind, the sadness making his eyes water.

The horseman took him into a beautiful red room that was plush with luxurious carpets and gold-framed pictures hung on the walls. Then, he pushed him into a small holding cell in a corner of the room, locked the door and threw a piece of bread at him, hitting him in the head.

"There's some food for you, you bloodthirsty bastard," he taunted, standing over him.

Suddenly the door swung open behind him. The horseman turned around quickly and knelt at the queen's feet. Then, he stood and met her gaze.

The Queen stood five feet ten inches. She was tall and slim with pale, smooth, skin, pure blond hair and wicked, piercing blue eyes; so wicked the evil radiated from them whether she liked it or not.

"You've brought him to me; you've done well," she muttered. "Now you can leave."

"What about the reward money, my Lady?"

Her eyes widened a little at his request. "Of course," she whispered. "Please refresh my memory. How much did I say I'd give you for his deliverance?"

"One hundred thousand dollars, my Lady," he said boldly.

There was a brief silence and then she withdrew a knife holstered in her waistband and stabbed him in the stomach.

Confusion marked his face as blood dripped from his mouth.

When she pulled out the blade out, he fell to the ground. She flipped her hair over her shoulder and laughed.

"You pawn, you peasant… One hundred thousand dollars," she mocked. Take him away now; he's spilling blood all over my carpet! Or be next," she spat.

When her cronies carried him away, she drew closer to Robert standing outside of the cage that held him captive. "So strong, but so weak," she said rolling her eyes across him as he sat on the floor.

"What do you want with me?" his weak voice uttered.

"Well, in a perfect world, I'd have you as my mate. I've heard about you and that girl of yours. What's her name," she muttered while snapping her finger, "oh, yeah – Beauty."

"Do whatever you want with me, but let her go."

She scoffed then, smiled arrogantly. "You know, I just might grant you that wish," she added, "but only because she is of no use to me. What I need from you is your blood Robert. Mixed with a little spell of mine, it will bring back to life all of the witches you've killed. First I must nurse you back to health; taking your blood now would be worthless. You're too weak," she said as someone knocked on the door and then entered.

It was the queen's daughter; a young dark-haired, pale-skinned, girl with beautiful green eyes. She was carrying a pitcher of lemonade, a cup and a plate of food.

"Just give it to him and leave, Lucille… Don't talk to him," she ordered as she left the room.

Then it was Lucille and Robert – all alone. She knelt down on her knees, grabbed the pitcher and poured the lemonade into his cup filling it to the brim.

The sound of it pouring reminded him of the creek downstream from the lake house and the way it burbled over the rocks.

She smiled and he smiled back. *She has a beautiful smile,* he thought, *the kind of smile that would brighten the sky like the sun on a cloudless day; not at all the kind you might expect from the daughter of an evil witch.*

She slid the tray that held his food underneath the bars then she stood up.

"Thank you," his faint voice whispered.

There was a brief silence as she stood motionless admiring how beautiful he was in person. She had heard so many stories about him. How he had bitten his way through the ranks and was the slayer of so many witches; not to mention how handsome he was.

"You're welcome," her soft, sincere voice said.

"You are such a beautiful sweet lady; so different from your mother. One wouldn't even know you were related." Robert said to her.

When he said that, she felt a chill shoot up her spine. His compliment made her smile but also made her more aware that she should leave, and fast.

She could still hear her mother's words replaying in her head before she left. "Just give it to him and leave." She knew her mother was probably right but his penetrating eyes held her still. He made her nervous – pleasurably nervous, so much in fact, that her hands began shaking. Shaking so much, she dropped the pitcher and it cracked open sending lemonade into the carpet.

"Oh, my mother is going to kill me," she said frantically as she knelt again and started picking up the shattered pieces and placing them into a cloth she was carrying. "Ouch – damn it," she blurted painfully as she cut her finger on a sharp piece of glass. She drew blood.

When the sweet scent of it hit the air, it hit his nostrils shooting a flicker of light through his eyes.

"I'm sorry, Lucille."

"For what?" she responded, flashing her eyes at him.

His eyes held her still with a deep stare crawling closer to the cage until his face was literally against the bars. "For having to compel you now," he said. "Stick your finger in my mouth and let me drink your blood; don't scream or, panic."

"OK," she nodded softly as she placed her finger in his mouth.

He sucked on it gently and began to feel the life and strength slowly creeping back into his body… His heart began to increase its beat, the veins beneath his eyes pulsated and finally his fangs emerged. The fact of the matter was that he'd have to drink her dry before he was back to full strength…

◆◆◆

In another room of the palace, Beauty had managed to get free and she bit her way through the ranks of guards, slaying them left and right. She increased her steps, speeding through the house looking for Robert.

◆◆◆

Meanwhile, Robert sucked on Lucille's finger like it was candy. He'd been at it for five minutes before his eyes blackened and his breathing grew heavier. His heart was pumping in his chest a little harder and he could feel his heightened senses returning. Then, he pulled her finger from his mouth.

"Why don't you be a doll and let me out of this cage." He suggested.

It took about thirty seconds before she'd grabbed the key from the wall and let him out.

Standing on the outside of the open cell, he lapped up every drop of blood that oozed from her finger.

Just then the queen pushed the doors open and stalked into the room. "No!" she screamed as Robert lifted his head and met her eyes.

Not a moment later Beauty appeared from behind her and slashed her fangs into the queen's neck, ripped her throat out, and then went after Lucille.

"No," Robert said holding her at bay. "Not her, love. Not her," he repeated.

When he let Lucille go, he wrapped his arms around Beauty and scattered kisses all over her. "I am so proud of you; you make me so happy, my lady."

"Likewise," she whispered, her beautiful smile filling her face.

"Now, make her forget what she saw, sweetheart; even the death of her mother," he added. Lucille doesn't deserve to live with that loss.

After Beauty compelled her, she and Robert walked out into the dark night and stood outside the palace for a moment.

Beauty thought of all the death she'd left scattered throughout the palace. Suddenly, they sensed something. They both turned around and looked back - there they saw the queen standing on the terrace behind them.

"She's not dead; how is that possible Robert?"

"That only means one thing, love. She's a hybrid, both vampire and witch and we didn't stake her in the heart," he said.

"You better run; both of you," she yelled out into the woods. "I'll hunt you down like dogs and kill you both."

There was a brief silence then Robert walked back towards the palace. He was quickly stopped by Beauty. "No," she said, "let us go and be happy now."

He rolled his eyes over her beautiful dark eyes and bronze skin. He nodded in agreement then glanced back at the terrace and said, "I admire your stubborn heart, queen; but sometimes you have to be big enough to realize how small you are... those are words of wisdom for you. Therefore, in addition to sparing your daughter's life, I will let you breathe tonight. But mark my words," he said. "Should you ever be stupid enough to hunt us again, I will rip your heart out of your chest and eat it myself; and you know I will," he added.

Then, Lucille stepped out on the terrace and looked at the queen strangely. "Who are you?" She asked.

"I'm your mother; don't be silly."

"You're not my mother," she blurted.

"Good night queen," Beauty laughed and flipped her hair over her shoulder.

"Yeah, good luck with that," Robert muttered sarcastically. Then he picked Beauty up in his arms, and leaped into the air.

To be continued...

Beyond Beauty: The beauty that lies beneath the surface of exterior beauty.

Strength, honor, intellect, love and compassion, the exercising of a moral compass towards others (mercy) these are just a fragment of the opinion that Robert for Beauty. It was his feeling toward her and, respectfully, it was her feeling toward him. From the death of her husband and years of loneliness, he came into her life and showed her that love was possible again. Beauty has the secret flame that will burn forever. But, is their journey of peace and love over, or will the queen have more to say about it?

End of Part 1

Beyond Beauty Part II Coming soon!

EMOTION STIRRED

She got the call on a warm summer's night as a gentle breeze blew across her on the terrace outside her suburban Manhattan mansion. She was wearing sheer, pearl-covered pajamas and was completely nude beneath. Her dark hair went across her face just before she drew it away. She could hear the palm trees swaying as the air drifted through its fronds. "Such a beautiful night," she thought wishing it wasn't spent alone. When she turned around and saw the fireplace crackling through a sliding glass door inside.

"Hello," she answered softly.

"Hey Stacy, it's Clifton. I know it's late and I hate to bother you, but uh… I got an interesting call at the office today and I thought you should know about it."

"Well," she said sarcastically as the wind blew into the phone distorting her hearing.

"Well, yeah, it was a guy named Suave calling from a Nevada correctional facility."

"I'm sorry Clifton, it sounded like you said correctional facility?"

He paused for a moment then continued. "Yeah, that's what I said, Stacy"

Her eyebrows rose curiously as the brief silence shook her nerves. "What did he say?" she asked.

He took a deep breath and then exhaled, dreading to be the bearer of bad news, "He said that you need to be on the next flight to Vegas so that you can visit him tomorrow… or…"

"Or what?"

"Or your life as you know it will be over."

"Well," she said giggling. "That's clearly the most bizarre request I've heard in a while!"

"You're right, Stacy. It is, but I think you should go."

"What!" she blurted. "Clifton, don't be ridiculous! He's probably just some con trying to get a rise out of me!"

"I know. It's just I've got a feeling about this guy."

The more she listened to Clifton, the more nervous she became. After all, he was her confidant, co-worker, and best friend with arguably greater intuition than hers.

"I just heard a determination in his voice Stacy. I think you should go check it out and see what he wants. He'll probably be in shackles anyway," he added.

"You really want me to fly all the way to Nevada to see some con in prison?"

After a few awkward moments he sighed then cleared his throat, "Yeah, I do Stacy." He sounded serious; dangerously serious. "Besides, we don't start filming again until Wednesday. Turn it into a vacation." He could hear her thinking a moment until finally she conceded.

"Alright, Clifton; but only because you're insisting it might be serious."

"Good girl; alright. I've gotta run now, Stacy; but ... uh ... call me when you get back."

"Will do."

When she hung up, she went inside and toasted some marshmallows in the fireplace and dropped a few in her cocoa, nibbling on another as it melted between her fingers and mouth.

Before calling it a night, she placed a call and made reservations for an early morning flight to go visit the convict at the prison.

The next morning, she boarded her flight at J.F.K. Airport on a non-stop flight to Vegas. Seated in business class, by 7:00am the plane had taken off and she had reclined in her seat.

She was wearing a white V-neck style T-shirt and tight dark jeans – her skinny jeans. Those jeans accentuated every curve on her long, seductive frame.

She was 5 foot 7 inches tall with long, dark hair flirting over her olive skin. Her dark, almond eyes were as mysterious as the ocean itself. People often told her she should be a model or something, but she knew her height wasn't necessarily as permitting. Besides, Stacy had other plans.

To those living under a rock, Stacy Landry is an American fashion consultant and media personality best known for her role on TV's "Manhattan Fashion," which broadcasts nationally on cable. She was born to Jewish-American parents on October 4th, 1979 and grew up without a doubt in New York. She was a New Yorker and everything about her said so.

She received her B.A. from Wells with a double major in psychology and philosophy. After college, she worked in the fashion industry first as an editor to several fashion magazines and later personally styling celebrities since 2006.

She worked on numerous advertising campaigns with just about every retailer. She loved to dress, but loved helping others project their inner beauty through outerwear even more.

With a yearly salary well in excess of $800,000, it is safe to say that she was certainly accustomed to the finest in life.

But even with such luxuries, she couldn't help be disturbed by the inconvenience of going to visit a stranger in prison; the thought of it disgusted her.

Her opinion of incarcerated people was that they all probably deserved to be in prison, and because she was coerced into going in the first place, it was beginning to serve as confirmation those thoughts.

She arrived at Las Vegas' McCarran airport six hours later and changed clothes in the ladies' room.

She knew that she was entering a world that was so far out of her comfort zone, she wanted to feel, and project, as much power as possible. She put on a black business suit that clung to her like a second skin. Just before she climbed into a black limousine, she pulled her hair in a pony tail.

She handed the driver a thousand dollars and asked if he could chauffeur her around for the day.

His eyes met hers in the mirror and he nodded his head slowly, releasing a crooked smile. "Uh, yes ma'am," he said "I'm at your service as long as you need."

She crouched down in the back of the limo, stretched her legs out and put on her dark designer sunglasses. "High Desert State Prison," she blurted, "that's where I need to go."

When she said that, the driver, a middle aged, heavy-set black man looked her over, more carefully this time. She's either a lawyer, or one of those chicks who likes roughnecks, he thought. After a few more moments of sizing her up, it dawned on him that she looked strangely familiar. "Excuse me, miss. Are you that lady from the TV show with the clothes – oh, what's the name of it?" he said, snapping his fingers trying to remember.

"Manhattan Fashion," she whispered.

"Yeah, yeah that's right! Manhattan Fashion! That's a very lovely show, ma'am. My wife watches it all the time."

She smiled at his enthusiasm even though she hated being recognized so quickly. Still, she found relaxation in his genuineness.

They drove for forty-five minutes then turned down a long, dirt road. When they pulled up to the prison gate there was a seriousness that swiftly came over her.

A tall, muscular guard stood at the entrance and ordered that all the windows be rolled down so he could see inside.

After a few moments, he made his way back to where she was sitting and looked inside. When he saw her, a strange look marked his face, as he immediately recognized her. But he didn't say anything. He gestured for the driver to full forward into the parking area.

Once they did, she told the driver she would be back in a few hours and to wait for her. Then, she got out of the limo and walked towards the entrance.

When she got inside, she was greeted by a young, blonde female officer behind a giant desk in the reception area. When she handed the officer her I.D. card, the woman looked back at her clearly recognizing her name.

"Oh my God! You're that celebrity lady, aren't you?"

"Shh," she playfully whispered, smiling as she nodded. "Yes, but I'm trying to be incognito."

"Oh yeah – I'm sorry," she replied, changing the subject by asking her who she was there to visit.

"Suave. I'm here to see Suave," she repeated.

There was an awkward silence as the officer returned her I.D. She noticed a change in the lady's demeanor but couldn't get a read off of it.

She was taken through a metal detector and then escorted to a room that looked like it was used for interrogations. "Is this where he's coming?" she asked nervously.

"No. He's actually in a similar room down the hall. We're gonna take you there in just a moment."

She could hear the static on the radio and a man's voice saying they were clear for movement. Her heart kicked up and began pounding in her chest as they walked down the hallway where he was being held. She noticed the further she walked, the more she realized just how dark of a place it was. She could hear yelling in the distance behind a steel gate which led down another dimly lit hallway. "Thank God I'm not going down that way," she thought. Then they came to a tall, dark, steel door and stopped.

"Okay, Ms Landry. Visits are 2 hours. In a moment, you'll go in and have a seat. He is in full restraints, but there is also a call button next to your chair in the event you need an officer, or you're ready to leave. Did you follow that, Ms. Landry?"

"Yeah, thanks," she nodded and then entered the room. The last thing she heard was the woman telling her to enjoy her visit just as the door closed behind her.

Now it was just her and him in this small space. She didn't make eye contact right away, but she could see him out of the corner of her eye. Finally she looked up.

When he saw her, he smiled and she smiled back, but her smile and his smile were two different smiles. The first thing he noticed was her posture. He knew what it represented. She was proud of herself and comfortable in her own skin. Stacy's deep beauty took Suave's breath away, still he acted unaffected. He turned on his charm and reminded himself of the objective.

"Wow, look who's here," he charmed greeting her with a smile. "Please, have a seat. Make yourself comfortable. I'm glad you could make it," he added.

No sooner than he said that, her seductive, almond-shaped eyes met his with frustration. She bit her lip to restrain a tart response. "It's not like you gave me much choice," she thought sarcastically. Then she quickly reminded herself to listen to what he had to say so she could get out of there.

He leaned back in his chair and stared at her, running his fingers through his long beard.

She flashed her dark eyes at him quickly then turned away before returning them again. It was the first time she'd looked at him completely. He was black and good looking in a way – that sought to shake her composure. He was tall, caramel and handsome. He had a long Egyptian silk looking beard that glistened over his light brown eyes. Strange, she thought. Those damn eyes of his are penetrating – an invasion of privacy somehow.

After a few seconds, she caught herself staring but concentrated on projecting a bland expression. When her eyes glanced down at his legs she could see the shackles around his ankles rubbing against the cemented pole in the floor that restrained his freedom.

"Can I offer you something to drink?"

Realizing he was in no such position to accommodate such a thing, his mordant humor compromised a smile as she consented to a smile. The sensation of his charm overwhelmed and scared her. She rolled her eyes trying to recover quickly as if it was to say she wouldn't give it to him.

"How's the weather outside, Stacy? I couldn't help but notice your glowing complexion."

"You didn't have me come all the way from New York to talk weather, did you?"

He smiled gently then shook his head. "Of course not; know what I mean?"

"No, I don't," she said as unfriendly as possible.

"Listen, lemme go this route with you," he directed with his tone hardening. "I know you aren't pleased that you had to leave your nice little life in Manhattan to come and see me here, but in a moment, you'll find out whether it was worth it," he added.

"Now, we're getting somewhere," she thought.

A few moments went by. He slowly ran his eyes over her body and up to her face. His eyes never left her. It was as if he examined her emotions for his amusement.

She could see him thinking and couldn't help but wonder what about.

"Well," he said, exhaling deeply. "I'm gonna ask you some questions and I need you to be honest with me, okay? When I'm done, I'll show you why you're here and we'll go from there."

"Yeah, let's get on with it," she blurted.

He sat up straight, pulled the notepad next to him closer and then adjusted the pen in his hand.

Are you the host of the TV show, "Manhattan Fashion?"

"Yes."

"Do you drink alcohol?"

"Yes."

"Smoke?"

"No."

"Do you find me attractive?"

There was a long pause at the end of that question, then her eyes met his. "No," she said sharply.

He scribed something down on the notepad and then flashed his eyes up at her.

"Did I say something wrong?" she asked.

Suave didn't answer. "Alright, one last question, Stacy."

"Praise the Lord," she said sarcastically.

"When was the last time you had sex?" he asked slowly – very, very slowly.

She sighed aggressively and shifted in her chair. "I'm not answering that question," she stated firmly.

"Stacy, it is one last question. Come on," he insisted rolling his eyes.

"Two years ago!" she blurted angrily. "Are you happy? Are you done now?" She didn't like revealing the answer to that question to him. It made her uneasy and gave him too much power being privy to such information. When she looked back up at him, she could see her answer didn't shock him - not at all and he never pressed her on it.

It wasn't until he finished that she realized his questions were more than just questions. He was learning from her; determining what she looked like when she was lying and what she looked like when she wasn't. But it was already too late.

He adjusted in his chair and appeared to be shifting gears.

"Alright, I've answered all your questions. Now show me what I'm here to see."

"You're a bitch, Stacy; you know that?"

"Well, at least we agree on something, Suave."

Then he shook his head and laughed to himself. "Yeah, but you're really not," he continued. "You use that as a defense mechanism to shield yourself from guys like me." His answer was so dead on she couldn't even respond at first.

"You're a rude boy," she said.

"Rude but smooth," he interrupted as he glanced at her French manicure. "Something I hear you New Yorkers are pretty fond of."

It didn't take a genius to see that Stacy was fascinated with Suave, though showing it was a different story. It had been a long time since she had met someone so beautiful and with an arrogance to match her own. He had a knowingness about him that was out of this world and as much as she hated to admit it to herself, it was simply true. He had a way of looking at you, placing thoughts right in your head. It was in that recognition, she visualized him pushing her around; making her do things she wouldn't normally do. Ripping her clothes off, pulling

165

her hair and spanking her from behind, whether she liked it or not.

He was a pretty boy but all man. He was mysterious with a dangerous look about him and it was that combination that fed her fascination amongst everything else about his powerful presence.

She remembered hearing that if you stared into his eyes long enough, he could hypnotize you. It was in that moment that he snapped his fingers to awaken her from a trance.

"Are you having a good time?" he asked with a crooked smile as if he'd witnessed every part of that fantasy.

Before she could even prepare a defense, he reached in his lap and slid a manila envelope across the table to her.

When it stopped in front of her, she met his eyes with a smile of relief. "He kept his word," she thought.

The he pulled on his beard, sat back and watched her. 'If you knew my power, you wouldn't smile at me, Stacy."

She rolled her eyes and dismissed the thought, hungry to see the contents of the envelope. She opened it and felt around before pulling out what felt like a stack of papers. When she looked closer, her heart fell to the pit of her stomach. She realized it was a stack of explicit photos of herself. Her eyes flared with both anger and disbelief. "How did you get these?" she asked.

"That's not important. What *is* important, is that these don't make it blazed across the inquirer.

To purchase: Emotions Stirred, go to Lulu.com

LOST WRITINGS OF VERNON NELSON VOL. 1

The Lost Writings of Vernon Nelson Vol. 2

My Life and My Charms…..Memoir

There are those who in their hardened heart's desire to hold me to a single mistake from my past; and forever and a day, to paint me in a ridiculous light. But, such a thing isn't just for any mortal, for all mortals are in error. There's not a person walking this planet without a past of regret that they'd like to be defined by.

I, Vernon Nelson, believe I have the right to redeem myself and produce my truth. So, in this book, I will declare mine…it is my belief that somehow it is connected to my destiny to experience what I've experienced. That somehow everything I've experienced, good and bad, has been all a part of the preparation for my spiritual awakening.

I was six years of age when God first spoke to me. It was the first time I felt his loving presence. He informed me that He had designed a special plan for me to carry out in my life. I am humbled to know that he had already considered my future follies that would eventually land me in prison and somehow still find me worthy to do his work in some version.

Many moons later, I stand before thee producing works from the fire he instilled within me that would never burn out. (My God-given talent). For I love the truth so much, I've often disguised it as a way of introducing it to those not conscious enough to accept it in it's purest form.

But, before my awakening, along the way are my follies, my experiences and my conquests. Discover the adventures of *My Life and My Charms.*

Available January, 2014 on Amazon.com

This book is a great gift for a friend or loved one who may either be incarcerated literally or, imprisoned by there own destructive concepts. Help them help themselves.

This book is dedicated to everybody in prison. To the forgotten… To all those who came before me and everybody in the struggle.

Peace and Love

God Bless.

I wanna thank everybody for your purchase. Please know that a percentage of all proceeds from this book (go to charity to help the hungry and less fortunate).

Vernon is clear about the purpose of this book:

I expect the open hearts, friendship, and respect of my readers, their open hearts; to give me an honest listen, their respect when they find I have more purpose than flaws; and their friendship should they find me worthy of it – my growth and core of character are of regal substance and transcend beyond the ordinary world. I extend my deepest apologies to anyone I may have ever offended.

LOST WRITINGS OPEN WITH...

My time in this prison building has served a great purpose for I have learned about myself and others. Never would I have imagined I'd be given a gift in the form of such oppression and that the pains of my confinement would give birth to such inspiration. It is here, I've learned the meaning behind God chastising the ones he loves. Before my arrival, I had traveled all around the world from Amsterdam to the U.K. Still, it was here I was forced to face myself and examine my flaws. It is in this dark place that I found light and reformed my way of thinking.

I share with you these intimate chapters from my journey in hopes it doesn't take you coming here before you meet change. However, in the event you do, remember this one thing - suffering is all a part of the great awakening.

Time is an illusion. Even this very moment is an illusion for in this second, you are receiving the distant thoughts from the inner-mystery of my mind; but only until this moment expires. And only as long as the flame of desire to discover the mysterious something that makes sense of life burns within, and only as long as you wish to unlock the doors of knowledge you've kept closed. Only then will I be able to offer you a greater sense of self and, god willing, ignite the divine sparks that leads to your spiritual awakening. It is the mission in life I've accepted.

I can promise throughout your reading you will experience great distractions from outer forces, they will most likely come from people the enemy's decided to use to hinder you from receiving this message; to keep you asleep – the state of mind that has brought you more sorrow than joy.

The laws of the spirit are funny this way for someone takes the time to bestow upon you precious knowledge only for someone else's attempt at silencing the messenger.

Now that you're aware of what is to come, I ask that you fasten your seatbelt and strap on your spiritual armor for this journey is both tireless and endless.

CHAPTER 1: Time Travelin'

When I used to close my eyes, I concentrated on the sound of each breath I took, listening carefully to the distinguished rhythm within me; each breath deeper and more elusive than the last. The more relaxed I became, the more the noise from inmates faded in the distance.

Several minutes went by as I lay still on the bottom bunk of my prison cell. It was late; I told myself twelve thirty something a.m. I recalled before my eyes shut - but that was then. For I had been lying still for so long that present time was nothing short of a mystery. I had finished saying my prayers when I noticed how quiet it was; too quiet, I thought.

My cellmate's snores around this time of night usually had me tapping the bottom of his bed so I could get him to shift and finally catch some sleep. But not this night; this night was different. For on this night, the quiet was incredible and the silence was piercing. As moments went on, I could feel my body relaxing; too much, I thought.

It was as if life itself was slowly leaving me. I tried desperately to panic; to muster up any strength I had to come up with to get free from wherever had its hold on me – but it was no use.

Paralyzed, I lay there helpless, watching myself fade into darkness. "I'm dying," I whispered faintly just as my spirit began drifting. The thought of departing earth for me was good and bad. Good because I'd finally reached a place in life where I believed heaven awaited me in the after-life; bad, because what happened next was even more strange.

Within seconds, a tingling sensation began pumping through me followed by a wave of brightness that held me still. After a few long moments, I found myself sitting upright, my eyes still closed despite how much I fought for their opening. It was as if a part of my conscience knew that I wasn't sleeping.

Next I felt being pushed back down - but it was a gentle touch and its power far greater than mine. I remember my body descending for what seemed like forever as it let me down softly.

By the time I hit the bed, the sound of fireworks were sounding off one after the other as flashing rays of light whisked rapidly through my bloodstream. I felt the euphoria brewing inside of me. And then, it happened - suddenly and without warning. I lay there suspended in time, somewhere between this life and the next.

The first thing I saw was green. There was a fluorescent gateway, sizzling as it turned, wheeling in a circular motion. I was briefly able to capture the image of someone gesturing for me to follow just before crossing over. Hesitating in my steps, I moved closer to the gateway marked by curiosity and gravitational pull, for there was something so right about the light – glistening behind the obscurity of fluorescence that drew my spirit toward it. Something so mysterious about this magical, spinning wheel, that willed me even closer.

To be honest, it pulled me inside, it's beautiful essence engulfed and wrapped around me. The last thing I remember was how beautiful and warm it was and bracing myself as I crossed over into the blur.

The time travel was quick; too quick, it seemed. It was like stepping through a sliding glass door and coming out on the other end. But when I opened my eyes, I simply couldn't believe them for they'd opened up into a strange realization. It was then I realized I had crossed into another dimension of time. And there I stood, in this foggy-misty-forest, searching, searching for any sign of life - existing I could find; any indication as to where I was and what was happening.

Finally, I began to walk, somewhere and anywhere, to find my way. I could hear the sound of an owl nearby and then it began to drizzle but that wasn't what affected me. It was the numbing of limbs and my running noise that worried me. How much of the cold could I bear I wondered.

The fog from each breath I took formed into thick clouds of smoke, puffing into the night's air.

Damn… it's foggy. I whispered icily. Shivering as a swift draft of air blew by me. Then, I caught a brief motion out of the corner of my eye but I couldn't make it out with clarity. I hesitated a few more steps then began listening with all my senses. I could sense someone was near; my senses told me so.

My eyes carefully glanced over the spacious forest but, my glances weren't enough to catch the swift shadow weaving between the trees. Every few seconds, I could see the flicker of gold sparks flying and then fading in the mist.

As the dark shadow swift through the underbrush of the forest, a tiny voice in the back of my mind reminded me to be calm. When the hairs on my arms stood, it wasn't human I told myself. And that was about all I was certain of. It had to have been moving at twice the speed of light I thought as I heard it breaking the air around me.

And then, it stopped abruptly. – Nothing but the sound of raindrops. My eyes wandered suspiciously seemed existent. After a few moments the fog began to clear.

The more I scanned the forest, the more hopeful I became of finding my way to some form of civilization. Then I saw something that took my breath away.

Just as the last bit of mist vanished into the air, I discovered a man standing there, off in the distance – his back was towards me.

"Hey," I yelled trying to capture his attention but to no avail. For he never once turned around or even acknowledged my presence. Still, seeing him was like an answered prayer I thought as a sense of relief came over me.

It wasn't long before I began walking across the forest towards him, very aware of my surroundings. The birds seemed to chirp louder with the more distance I closed between us almost as if a warning. But to whom, I wondered. To him, or I?

After a few more steps, I realized that this man wasn't just any man. For this man had a white and gold outline glistening around him, I realized that his very appearance was non human – ghost like. It was as if a hologram or spirit was standing before me.

All of a sudden, a flicker of his image shot through the forest like a bullet in the wind. The light from the heat waves glittered in purple and sparkles from how fast he cut through the air.

I couldn't believe my eyes. I awed as I stood in amazement. I spotted him when he reappeared several feet ahead just as he began walking; very slowly I recalled. He was weaving between the trees headed toward something important.

I could tell by the determination in his steps that he wanted me to follow him. I could sense it.

Perhaps the most intriguing part of that recognition was that he never asked or even spoke. For that matter, it was just a feeling that seemed to radiate from him – a signal of some sort.

And so, I followed as he led me through the forest to a destination unknown. Every few moments, he'd stop and wait for me before he continued. The mind boggling thing about it was I remember telling myself how incredibly slow he was walking. Still, no matter how fast I moved, my brisk motions couldn't keep up with his delayed, faint steps.

And then the very dimension of time in which I stood began to change right before my eyes. The gray clouds turned electric blue as purple and pink sparkles drizzled from the sky down to the wet forest floor. But that lasted briefly for after a few seconds, several transforming images flickered rapidly; one moment it was a tribe of men spearing a surrounded lion in the African safari and the next, I was standing in the Egyptian desert. I could see the pyramids in the distance with guards overseeing slaves who were carrying enormous stones toward it. It was simply unbelievable.

My eyes glistened at the sight of the spacecraft hovering over and assisting in the creation of the pyramids.

The last image I witnessed was the transition to a tall glorious mountain and standing on top of it. It overlooked a series of transforming moments in millions of protective bubbles.

For it was like starring into the mystery of time itself; to say I was speechless would be an understatement because the truth is, I was utterly breathless. My eyes slowly scanned over the images and the more I did, the more I realized just exactly what I was looking at. I sighed briskly in admiration of the moment.

The gray clouds over the brown, rocky mountains were barely visible as a cold breeze swift across me shaking me to the core.

To my right, stood the man I'd been following all along, only this time, I was standing directly beside him and he didn't make eye contact. His attention was focused on the life images playing out in the protective bubbles beneath us.

The random images from B.C., A.D. and times I couldn't make out flashed swiftly. Like destined, written imagery, there were different people and events from the past, present, and some presumed to be of the future.

When my eyes rolled across him, I realized how strangely familiar he looked - as if I'd seen this man before. His gold skin glistened over his long white beard. "Why are you showing me this," I reluctantly whispered.

Not a moment later, he shushed me.

What I found absolutely amazing was how the thunder roared when he did that. Even the mountains were humbled as they began cracking. It was then he turned towards me.

Finally, I would look into the eyes of the man I'd followed into this mysterious time and place. But before I could even see his eyes, mine were met with blinding rays of light and an overwhelming power rippled through me as if it were instilling something inside me.

It held me still a while longer, rocking me deeper and pushing past any boundaries of control I thought existed. It was the most beautiful sensation I'd ever felt in my life. It continued for what seemed like forever and then a calm reassuring voice spoke to me – the voice of the Almighty. And he directed that I give you this Message.

Purchase The Lost Writings of Vernon Nelson @ www.lulu.com

Emotion Stirred go to www.lulu.com

Author Vernon Nelson delivers masterful storytelling in Beyond Beauty and Emotion Stirred. Two masterpiece romance novels that will leave you breathless. The Lost Writings of Vernon Nelson, the self-help book, will explain the ancient power within you.

Emotion Stirred and The Lost Writings books are available at:

http://www.lulu.com

Join the Phenomenon!

ABOUT THE AUTHOR

 Vernon Nelson was born in England in 1979 to Vernon Sr. and Miss Charlotte. He was raised from the Netherlands and Germany to the United States. He has traveled to many countries including Italy, France, Sweden and Belgium, to name a few. Since he can remember, he has always vibrated with various forms of artistry and has had an appetite for knowledge. As a teenager he toured with artists on their European tours, such as Wu-Tang's Capadonna, and then later formed a group entitled "Legacy". Here he performed and co-wrote several songs with his father.

As time went on, he continued to write, perfecting his craft while embarking on a quest of enlightening spiritual studies. "I find purpose and meaning to life," he says touching others with his heartfelt, life-changing stories. "I am fascinated with the mystery of time, faith and human will."

Vernon's transition from artist to author took place in his untimely incarceration in 2002. His inquisitive mind in prison fueled the flame of his desire. "To find myself," he says "and to enlighten and help others find themselves; it is one of my personal necessities of life."

Wise beyond his years, Vernon authored *Emotion Stirred.* An inmate mind-challenging romance novel, guaranteed to captivate and keep you on edge. Manhattan's fashion guru celebrity, Stacy Landry, is summoned from the leisure of her luxurious life to meet a man in prison often heard about, but never seen (Mr. Suave)...but it's his intentions and the mind challenging ride in which locked doors are pried open and masks are revealed.

Relationships will be tested, boundaries will be pushed past and emotions will be stirred all for a suspenseful journey leading to an ending that will leave your breathless.